BUFFALO BILL'S LAST SHOW?

The applause for Cody continued. Clint saw the Lutzes clapping their hands—Philip Lutz somewhat halfheartedly—and also Lieutenant O'Grady.

And then he saw that man again. He still didn't know where he'd seen him from, only that he was familiar. The other odd thing was that the man was not clapping. He was simply staring up at Cody on the stage—then Clint saw the gun and knew he had to act fast.

He leapt up onto the stage, to the surprise of Cody and the crowd.

"Clint, what the—" Cody said, but Clint hit him just as the shot rang out, both cutting him off.

Clint and Cody fell to the ground together and the crowd was shouting. Clint looked down at Cody and saw the blood.

"He's been shot," he said. "Colonel Cody's been shot."

DON'T MISS THESE
ALL-ACTION WESTERN SERIES
FROM THE BERKLEY PUBLISHING GROUP

THE GUNSMITH by J. R. Roberts
Clint Adams was a legend among lawmen, outlaws, and ladies. They called him . . . the Gunsmith.

LONGARM by Tabor Evans
The popular long-running series about U.S. Deputy Marshal Long—his life, his loves, his fight for justice.

McMASTERS by Lee Morgan
The blazing new series from the creators of Longarm. When McMasters shoots, he shoots to kill. To his enemies, he is the most dangerous man they have ever known.

SLOCUM by Jake Logan
Today's longest-running action Western. John Slocum rides a deadly trail of hot blood and cold steel.

THE GUNSMITH

162

THE LAST GREAT SCOUT

J. R. ROBERTS

JOVE BOOKS, NEW YORK

THE LAST GREAT SCOUT

A Jove Book/published by arrangement with
the author

PRINTING HISTORY
Jove edition/June 1995

ISBN: 0-515-11635-1

A JOVE BOOK®
Jove Books are published by The Berkley Publishing Group,
200 Madison Avenue, New York, New York 10016.
JOVE and the "J" design are trademarks
belonging to Jove Publications, Inc.

PRINTED IN THE UNITED STATES OF AMERICA

10 9 8 7 6 5 4 3 2 1

THE GUNSMITH
162

THE LAST GREAT SCOUT

ONE

Clint Adams looked down at Helen Slate as she slept peacefully on her back. Lately, whenever he was going to bed with a woman, Clint caught himself watching her—while she undressed, while she slept, while she dressed again—hell, even during sex. He hadn't noticed it before the past few months, but when he was making love to women he had started watching them, observing their reactions, their facial expressions . . .

For instance, during this night Helen had been on top of him, sitting on him, his penis buried deep inside of her. Her hands had been pressed to his belly and she was working herself up and down on him. Now, this had happened many times in the past and he had found himself more often than not with his eyes closed, just experiencing his own pleasure. Oh, sure, once in a while he'd open his eyes and look at the woman, or touch her—but you didn't need to have your eyes open to find a woman's breasts with your hands. And very often the room was dark, so you wouldn't see much anyway.

This night, however, he had left the lamp lit, turned low, but bright enough for him to see her. He had watched her as she rode him, enjoying the way she squeezed her eyes closed, liking the way she bit her bottom lip, appreciating the line of her throat when she tossed her head back . . .

Now he stared down at her as she slept. The bed sheet had slipped just low enough to show her cleavage, which was impressive. For a woman in her early thirties, she had marvelous breasts, big, firm, rounded undersides. He reached over and tugged the sheet a little lower without waking her, exposing her brown nipples. They were flattened now, but when she was excited and they were distended they stood out longer than any he'd ever seen before.

Clint thought about touching them, with a finger, with his tongue, but instead he got up from the bed and walked to the window. His legs felt weak, because he and Helen had spent most of the night making love.

He looked outside, down at the street. It was still dark, but daylight was not far away. He would be leaving Denver in the morning, taking a train to Chicago. He'd been here for about four days, the last two spent with Helen, who worked in the hotel where he was staying. She was the manager of the restaurant in the lobby. The day he arrived he ate dinner there and she had come over to make sure he was satisfied with everything. Later she told him that she saw him from the kitchen and just had to come over and speak to him. It was not until the third day, however, that he had asked her to join him for a meal somewhere away from the hotel, and she had accepted. That night they went to bed, and he allowed her to entice him to stay an extra day.

Clint had a friend waiting for him in Chicago, a man named Eaton who was a writer. He had been invited by letter at a time when a long train trip appealed to him. He had ridden Duke, his big, black gelding, to Denver, where the horse would remain while Clint was in Chicago. He had a friend here in Denver, a professional investigator named Talbot Roper, who would be watching over Duke for him.

"What's in Chicago?" Roper had asked during lunch that first day.

"A friend."

"A woman?"

Clint smiled and shook his head.

"A man."

"Been to Chicago before?"

"Never for any length of time," Clint said. "I'm actually looking forward to seeing the city."

"It's a great city," Roper said. "I've often thought about relocating there."

"What's stopping you?"

"Moving my files," Roper said.

"If that's stopping you, then I guess you don't really want to go," Clint said.

It was Roper's turn to smile as he said, "No, I guess not . . ."

Clint would have liked to have spent more time with Helen, but Mark Eaton was waiting for him in Chicago. As it was, he'd be arriving a day late.

He turned as Helen stirred on the bed, moaning.

She stretched in her sleep, arching her back and pointing her toes. The sheet slipped away and he looked at her belly, her thighs, her buttocks as she turned onto her side, her back to him now.

He smiled.

"You're awake, aren't you?" he asked.

There was a moment's hesitation and then she said, "Yes."

"You're a tease, you know that, don't you?"

There was a soft laugh and then she said, "Come back to bed and I'll show you that I can do more than tease."

It was an offer he couldn't refuse.

TWO

Later that morning Talbot Roper came by in a buggy and gave Clint a ride to the train station.

"How was your night?" Roper asked.

"It was fine."

"Restful?"

"Not really."

"I didn't think so," Roper said. "You look like hell."

"Thanks."

"Still, I suppose you can sleep on the train, right?"

"Right."

Clint thought about Helen then. It would have been a waste to sleep too much of the night, considering what they had been doing when they were awake . . .

She watched him dress to leave, still naked on the bed herself, with the sheet on her.

"When will you be back this way?"

"I have to come back for my horse," he said, strapping on his gun. "I'll let you know when I get here."

"That's flattering," she said. "Come for your horse and make time for me." She spoke without rancor.

Clint smiled at her and said, "I've known my horse longer than I've known you."

"I suppose you have," she said, "but I bet he's never done for you what I do."

"You've got a point there."

When he was fully dressed, she asked, "Are you sure you have to leave?"

"I'm a day late as it is," he said.

"Well," she said, "I guess I'll have to be content with that, won't I? At least I made you a day late."

"Yes, you did."

He leaned over to kiss her and as his lips met hers she tossed the sheet away. He ran his hand over her body, from her breasts over her belly to her crotch, where he touched her gently.

"Ooh," she said, squeezing her thighs together, trapping his hand there, "who's the tease now?"

"I need that hand," he said, and she opened her warm thighs.

He walked to the door, carrying his grip, then turned to look at her.

"I will let you know when I'm back, Helen."

"I know you will," she said. She reclined on the bed, the sheet on the foot. She put her hands behind her neck, which lifted her beautiful breasts. "I'm not worried."

He laughed, opened the door, and left to find Roper waiting for him downstairs . . .

• • •

"How long are you going to be in Chicago?" Roper asked.

"I don't know. I guess it depends on how much I like it."

"If that's the case," Roper said, "you might never be back."

"Oh, I'll be back," Clint said. "I tend to enjoy these big cities for a while, but I generally get homesick. Besides, I've got to come back and get Duke."

"I was kind of hoping you'd like it where you were and send me a telegram telling me to keep the big brute."

"Dream on."

Roper dropped Clint at the station but did not wait for the train to leave.

"I've got an early appointment."

"I figured you didn't get up early just to see me off," Clint said.

The two friends shook hands and Clint got out of the buggy.

"Let me know when you're coming back," Roper said.

"I'll send you a telegram."

"Oh, before you go." Roper reached into his pocket and handed Clint a plain white envelope with a name and address on it.

"Will you deliver that for me?"

"Sure."

"I mean hand deliver it, not put it in the mail," Roper said.

Clint looked at it, shrugged, and said, "Yeah, sure."

"Don't you want to know what it is?"

"None of my business," Clint said, tucking the envelope away. "You want it delivered, I'll deliver it."

"I appreciate it."

They shook hands again and Clint walked to the front of the station and opened the door. Behind him he heard Roper's horse clip-clopping away. Fleetingly, he touched the envelope he had put inside his jacket, then shrugged and went into the station. Curious as he might be, what he told Roper was actually the way he felt. What was in the envelope was not his business.

Still, once he was seated he took the envelope out and held it up to the window. There seemed to be a piece of paper inside with typewritten lines on it. A letter. So what? The name on the front was Mr. James Hannigan, and the address was on Rush Street. The name meant nothing to him. He put the envelope back into his pocket with intentions of forgetting about it, and stared out the window as the train started to move.

THREE

When Clint got off the train in Chicago, he had no idea that his life was going to intersect with that of a man who was in a room in a fleabag Rush Street hotel.

The man was a killer. He had killed in many cities and states across the country, and he did so not because he was hired to, and not because he liked to. He did it because he was told to.

By a voice . . .

Inside his head . . .

Right at that moment he was sitting on the bed in his room, listening to the voice. It was telling him who to kill, and where to find him. The man nodded as the voice spoke, then opened his eyes and picked up the newspaper that was lying there. Right on the first page, as the voice had said, he saw the name of his intended victim.

Clint got off the train in Chicago and bought a copy of *The Chicago Tribune* to read in his hotel. On

the front page he saw an announcement that Buffalo
Bill Cody was going to be in town. Clint had never
met Cody, but his friend Wyatt Earp had spoken very
highly of the man as a scout and a buffalo hunter.
Now Cody was a showman, and apparently doing
very well.

In a cab to his hotel, the Drake, Clint read the ar-
ticle on Cody. Apparently the man's famous "Wild
West" show was not with him, but he was going to
be having some speaking engagements. Clint decided that he'd stop by one of them to meet Cody,
invoking the name of Wyatt Earp if he had to.

Mark Eaton had promised Clint a reservation at
the Drake, and was true to his word. Clint was immediately whisked to his room by a bellman who
carried his bag. There was a bathtub in the room and
Clint made use of it, soaking bones that were tired
from long hours of sitting on a train. Sometimes he
thought that sitting on a seat in a train for hours was
worse than sitting on a horse for a long period of
time.

He soaked in the tub for an hour, reading every
word of the newspaper he had bought. There was little in it, however, that was of as much interest to
him as the story on Buffalo Bill Cody. He went back
to it and found the schedule of Cody's speaking engagements. The first one was the following afternoon, at some men's club on Huron Street. Later, he
would find out that the club was walking distance
from his hotel.

After his bath he dressed in fresh clothes. His intention was to deliver his friend Roper's letter, then
find out where the men's club was that Cody would
be speaking at. He pulled on his boots and then, be-

fore leaving the room, completed his wardrobe by tucking his little New Line Colt in his belt, at the small of his back. More than once the little belly gun—or small-of-the-back gun—had saved his life. He chose not to wear his holster when he was in a city with a police department that frowned on it, and the New Line kept him from feeling naked.

He left the room and went down to the plush lobby of the Drake hotel. Before leaving he decided to go into the hotel bar and have a cold beer.

The bar was as plush as the rest of the hotel, with a long mahogany bar, gold-plated fixtures, crystal chandeliers and leather-covered chairs—most of which were taken up by prosperous-looking men in business suits. The Drake was a high-class establishment, one Clint would not have chosen to stay in of his own accord.

He went up to the bar and ordered a beer. The bartender was a young man with muttonchops that looked grossly out of place on his face.

"Thanks," Clint said when the bartender set down his drink.

"Sure."

Clint took a sip and then asked the bartender, "Can you tell me where this place is?" He pointed to the address in the newspaper but read it aloud anyway. "The Huron Gun and Hunt Club?"

"Oh, sure, you can walk there from here," the bartender said, and proceeded to give him the proper directions. "You could get a cab there easy, but it's only a few blocks away."

"Thank you."

As Clint took another swallow of beer, the man leaned his elbows on the bar and asked, "Are you going there to hear Mr. Cody?"

"That's right," Clint said. "He and I have some friends in common."

The man's eyes widened and he stood up straight and stared at Clint.

"You know friends of Colonel Cody?"

"That's right."

"You mind me asking you where you're from, mister?" the man asked.

"Out west. I just got into Chicago and this beer tastes mighty good."

He finished it and pushed the empty mug across the bar to the man.

"Would you like another?"

"I don't think—"

"On the house, of course," the man added quickly. "As a welcome to Chicago?"

"Well . . . when you put it that way, sure."

The bartender eagerly drew another beer and set it in front of Clint.

"Mister, can I ask your name?"

Clint sipped from the beer and put it down.

"Sure, why not? It's Clint Adams."

Now the young man's eyes widened again, and Clint suddenly wished he hadn't been so free to answer the question.

"Are you *the* Clint Adams?"

Clint was surprised that someone here in Chicago would recognize his name. It never failed to surprise him how many places he was known.

"I'm the only Clint Adams I know of."

Now he was eager to finish his beer and get away from the bartender's enthusiasm. In fact, maybe he wouldn't even finish the beer . . .

The younger man reached beneath the bar and came out with a book. A dog-eared, wrinkled book that had been read many times and had the name THE GUNSMITH in the title. Clint recognized it. It was one of the dime novels that had been written a long time ago by a writer in New York. The first time Clint ever saw them—and there were several—he had traveled to New York to put a stop to it. Every once in a while, though, one of them jumped up and bit him on the ass.

Like now.

FOUR

"Are you this Clint Adams?" the man asked anxiously, pointing to the book. "The Gunsmith?"

"That's right."

"Oh . . . gee!" the man said. "Imagine that. Two in one day!"

"Two . . . what does that mean?" Clint asked.

"Well, first Colonel Cody shows up in my bar, and now you."

"Buffalo Bill was here?" Clint asked, surprised.

"Oh, yes, sir. The colonel is staying in this hotel. Didn't you know?"

"No, I didn't."

"Well, yes, sir, he is—and he's here right now."

"In the hotel?"

The bartender leaned across the bar and said, "In the bar. There's some private rooms in the back and the colonel and some people are in one of them."

Clint looked toward the back of the room.

"You don't say."

"Yes, sir, I do. Why don't you go back there and say hello?"

Clint smiled and said, "I wouldn't want to interrupt the colonel if he's doing business."

"I bet he wouldn't call it an interruption if he knew you were the Gunsmith himself."

"That may be, but I think I'll wait—"

"Excuse me, sir," a voice said behind him.

Clint turned and saw a man in an expensive three-piece suit, holding a bowler hat in his hand and reeking of an equally expensive scent.

"Can I help you?"

"I couldn't help but overhear as I entered," the man said. "Am I to understand that you are Clint Adams, the Gunsmith?"

"My name is Clint Adams, yes."

"Well, sir, allow me to introduce myself." The man extended his hand. "My name is Howard Billings."

"What can I do for you, Mr. Billings?"

Clint reclaimed his hand and wondered if it was going to smell like the scent the man was wearing. He resisted lifting it to his nose and sniffing.

"Well, sir, I happen to be a representative of the Huron Gun and Hunt Club—in fact, several of the prominent men's clubs around the city. It was I who arranged the speaking engagements of Colonel Cody."

"I see," Clint said. "I'm sure that must have been a feather in your cap, Mr. Billings."

"Indeed, it was," Billings said happily. "I was wondering, sir, if we might convince you to join Colonel Cody—"

Clint waved the man off immediately.

"I don't think so, Mr. Billings."

"May I ask why not?"

"I'm here on private business and don't relish the idea of calling attention to myself."

"Yes, but—"

"Besides, Colonel Cody might not like the idea of sharing the, uh, spotlight."

"I'm sure he wouldn't mind, if he knew who he'd be sharing it with."

"Mr. Billings—"

"Why don't we ask him?"

"I don't think—"

"I happen to be on my way to join him. Would you accompany me as my guest?"

Clint hesitated. He did want to meet Cody, and where would the harm be? After all, he had no intention of accepting the offer from Howard Billings, therefore he'd be no threat to Cody.

"All right, Mr. Billings," he said, "why don't you lead the way?"

FIVE

The back rooms were separated from the rest of the bar by curtains, not doors. Billings led Clint to one of those curtained doorways.

"Wait here a moment, please," he said, and slipped through the curtain. Clint could hear him speaking very clearly.

"Excuse me, gentlemen, but I have someone outside who would like to see you, Colonel Cody."

"The colonel does not have time for fans right now, Billings—" a raspy-voiced man started, but something cut him off.

"Who is it, Mr. Billings?" another voice asked. Clint assumed this to be Cody. He found the voice of the showman to be remarkably soft.

"His name is Clint Adams, sir. You might know him better as—"

"The man needs no further introduction, Mr. Billings," Cody said, his tone rising. "Don't keep the man waiting outside. Bring him in here."

17

Hastily, the curtains were parted and Billings's face appeared, looking pale and sweaty.

"Come in, Mr. Adams, come in."

Clint stepped through the curtains and found himself in a small room that was virtually all table. If the curtains were drawn, the table would quickly become part of the other room. For now, it was hidden away and there were four men seated at it.

Well, three of them were seated and one—William F. Cody—was standing.

"By God, man, it's years I've been looking forward to meeting you."

He thrust his hand out and Clint grasped it and shook it with equal pleasure.

"I admit to the same, Colonel Cody."

"Wyatt Earp has told me much about you, Mr. Adams, and years ago Jim Hickok had nothing but good things to say about you."

"I'm glad to hear that, Col—"

"Forget that 'Colonel' stuff," Cody said. "You call me Bill. Sit down, Clint, sit down. Billings, get Clint whatever he wants."

Clint sat down, looked up at Billings, and said, "A beer will be fine."

Clint looked around the table and saw that the other men were studying him dubiously. He had the distinct feeling that none of them had recognized his name the way Buffalo Bill Cody had.

"Gentlemen, stop staring," Cody said. "Don't you know who this man is?"

The three men looked at Cody, and then at each other. Clint took the time to study each of them.

The man on his immediate left was white-haired, well dressed, and, when standing, Clint guessed he would go about sixty-five inches or so. His face was pink and lined, but his eyes were blue and startlingly clear for a man who was obviously in his sixties.

To his immediate right was a tall man, very slender, with dark hair combed straight back and slicked with pomade. His face was angular and he wore carefully manicured chin whiskers that could barely be called a beard. His eyes were a muddy brown that Clint distrusted on sight.

Sitting across the table, next to Cody, was a man in his twenties, not as well dressed as the other two. His brown hair was lank and lifeless, while next to him Cody's blond mane flowed majestically.

Cody himself was dressed as if for a show. A buckskin jacket with fringe, gloves on the table next to his drink. A blue chambray shirt underneath the jacket. Cody himself, even seated in this atmosphere, looked like the ultimate showman. His hair and beard were clean, well-groomed, and his eyes were shining with enthusiasm, whether for meeting Clint or simply for life Clint didn't know. Cody, for all his exploits and reputation, was not yet forty years old.

"This gentleman is Clint Adams."

"We heard that, Bill," the man with the angular face said.

Cody looked at the man next to him.

"Surely you've heard of Clint Adams, Jerald."

Jerald looked at Cody and obviously wanted to impress the man.

"He was a good friend of Hickok's," Cody said.

"Is that a recommendation, Bill?" said the man with the angular face. "We were doing business here—"

"And now we're not, Derek," Bill Cody said, cutting the man off. "You don't know who you're sitting here with."

"Why don't you tell me?" Derek said.

"Bill—" Clint said, wanting to keep the man from saying anything embarrassing.

"Just let me tell these uninformed fools who you are, Clint," Cody said. The man seemed genuinely upset that the other three men didn't know who Clint was.

"Gentlemen, allow me to introduce you to the Gunsmith himself."

Clint winced at the introduction.

"Ah," Cody said, with satisfaction,"I see you all know that name, don't you?"

"The Gunsmith?" repeated the angular-faced Derek. "Sir, it's a genuine pleasure to meet you." He put his hand out, which Clint took but quickly relinquished. The man had a grip like a wet bar rag.

"My name is Derek Mills, Mr. Adams. I run a theater here in town, a very fine theater at which Colonel Cody will be performing—"

"If we can come to terms," Cody said, cutting the man off.

"Ah, yes," Mills said. "You see, Mr. Adams, that's what we were discussing when you came in."

"I'm sorry I interrupted," Clint said, as Billings appeared with his beer. "I can leave—"

"Nonsense," Cody said, waving his hand. "We can discuss business later, Derek. I have an opportunity now that I have been looking forward to for a long time, and I'm not about to pass it up. What say you, gentlemen?"

Cody looked at each man in turn, daring them to disagree.

"Whatever you say, Bill," the white-haired man said. "Actually, Derek and I can take this discussion elsewhere while you talk to Mr. Adams here."

"That's a fine idea, Ed," Cody said. "Clint, this is Edward Blaylock. He's been booking some of my appearances in the east and the midwest. Derek, is that all right with you?"

"Whatever you say, Bill. If you're willing to let Ed negotiate, that's fine by me."

"Excellent. Then you two can get out and leave us alone."

Both men stood up to leave.

"Take your drinks," Cody said.

They picked up their drinks.

"It was a pleasure to meet you, Mr. Adams," Derek Mills said. "I hope to get the chance to talk to you again soon. Will you be in Chicago long?"

"A few days."

"Fine, fine," Mills said.

Ed Blaylock simply nodded to Clint and followed Mills out of the room.

"Bill, should I—"

"You stay where you are, Jerald. Clint, this young fellow is Jerald Wilkins."

"Hello, Jerald."

"Hello, sir. It's a pleasure to meet you."

Clint could see now that Wilkins was closer to twenty than he had originally thought.

"You see this man, Jerald?" Cody said. "This is the closest you will get to Wild Bill Hickok ever. Even when Jim was alive there was some question as to who the better man was with a gun."

"Not in my mind, there wasn't," Clint said. "There wasn't a better man anywhere, anytime with a gun than James Butler Hickok."

"By God," Cody said, picking up his drink, "I'll drink to that!"

The three of them lifted their drinks and did just that.

SIX

"What brings you to Chicago, Clint?" Cody asked when their toast was done.

"Personal business," Clint said. "I'm here to see a friend."

"Well, whatever brings you here I'm grateful for it," Cody said. "I thought Chicago was going to be dull."

"What brings you here? Performing?"

"Not really. We've just returned from Europe, where we performed for royalty, and now I'm gathering some people together for an extended hunting trip through the West. We'll be starting from North Platte, Nebraska. I don't suppose I could entice you to join us?"

"I don't know," Clint said. "When are you planning to leave?"

"A few days, I hope, just as soon as the remainder of my party gets here. Young Jerald, here, is going to write about it. Aren't you, boy?"

"That's right."

"Tell Clint the title you've come up with."

Wilkins cleared his throat and said, " 'A Thousand Miles in the Saddle with Buffalo Bill.' "

"It's catchy," Clint said. "I guess it would depend on whether or not my business was complete when you were ready to leave."

"Well, why don't we just stay in touch, then?" Cody said.

"That's fine."

"In fact, why don't you come and hear me speak tomorrow at this, uh, Gun and Hunt Club. I understand it's just around the corner from here."

"I might do that, if I have the time. I have to meet my friend—"

"Bring him with you. God knows, I perform better the bigger the crowd."

"I'll keep it in mind, Bill."

"Well . . . good. Listen, can you join me for dinner tonight? I'd like to liven up the conversation around the table."

"Uh, I can't tonight. I have some errands to run."

"Oh, too bad," Cody said, obviously disappointed. "Well, perhaps tomorrow night, after my talk."

"Perhaps. Uh, how many performances will you be putting on while you're here?"

"As many as I can book. The rest of my little troupe is not here, but I have to keep myself in the public eye, don't I?"

"I suppose you do, if you want to keep doing what you're doing."

"I do," Cody said. "Some call it flamboyant foolishness, but I like it."

"From what I hear, a lot of people like it."

"Oh, let me tell you," Cody said, his eyes shining, "they ate it up in Europe. England, France, Germany, they all loved it. Have you seen my show, Clint?"

"I can't say that I have, Bill. I'm sorry."

"After this hunting trip we'll start playing again, and you'll be my guest."

"It would be an honor."

"Listen," Cody said, "have you ever thought about going on stage yourself?"

Clint had been on stage briefly in St. Louis, as an actor, when he was trying to help catch a killer, but he knew Cody meant as himself, talking about his exploits.

"No, I haven't."

"Jim did it, you know."

He meant Hickok.

"I know," Clint said, "and from what I heard he hated it."

"Maybe," Cody said, "but that was Wild Bill. He wasn't at his best on stage in front of a theater full of people. You, on the other hand, might be a different story."

"I don't think so, Bill."

"Well, I saw the look in Derek Mills's eye. He's going to try to get you to do it while you're here."

"He won't succeed."

"Well, if he doesn't," Cody said, "maybe you'd consider coming to work for me?"

Clint sat back.

"That's a flattering offer, Bill, but—"

"Don't answer me now, Clint," Cody said. "Think about it for a while."

"I will, Bill," Clint said. "I promise. Unfortunately, I've got an errand to run right now, but it's been a real pleasure to meet you."

He stood up and they shook hands again.

"I'll see you at one of my shows," Cody said. "Maybe watching me make a fool of myself will help you make up your mind."

"I'll be there," Clint promised, "but I don't think I'll be changing my mind."

"That'll be up to you," Cody said. "I'm just making the offer. I'm not going to pressure you."

"I appreciate that, Bill. I expect I'll be seeing you sometime tomorrow."

"I look forward to it."

Clint turned and left Cody and his young friend, slipping through the curtain into the main area of the bar. Meeting Cody had been an unexpected pleasure, but being offered a job in his show was even more unexpected—though it was not especially tempting. He had done some sharpshooting briefly in the past, while people watched, but the idea of putting himself on display day in and day out in Cody's show was not the least bit attractive to him.

Flattering though—very flattering.

SEVEN

As Clint was about to leave the bar, he heard some-one call his name and turned to find Derek Mills bearing down on him.

"Could I talk to you for a moment?"

"I thought you were doing business with Mr. Blaylock."

"Oh, we've come to terms. It wasn't hard once I got Blaylock away from Colonel Cody."

"Is Colonel Cody a shrewd negotiator?"

"He's a storyteller," Mills said. "Before you can make a deal with him, you've got to listen to count-less stories about his exploits."

"Isn't that the kind of thing you pay him for?"

Mills smiled.

"Yes, but it gets in the way during business ne-gotiations—which is what I want to talk to you about."

"I have an errand to run . . ." Clint said lamely.

"It will only take a moment, I assure you."

"Well . . . all right."

"Can I buy you a drink?"

"I don't think so, Mr. Mills. As I said, I am in a bit of a hurry."

"All right, then," Mills said, "I'll get right to it. I'd like you to perform at my theater while you are here in Chicago."

"I don't think so."

Mills gave him an exasperated look and said, "You haven't even heard my offer."

"I don't have to. I don't perform."

"All you have to do is tell stories—"

"I don't tell stories, Mr. Mills. I'm afraid you're just out of luck."

"I can pay you quite a bit of money, Mr. Adams."

"Mr. Mills," Clint said, "I really do have to go and run my errand."

"Well, you go ahead, then. Think about it. We can talk about it later."

"There's nothing to talk about."

"In negotiations there is always something to talk about, Mr. Adams," Mills said, and walked away before Clint could comment.

He left the hotel, pleased that he had met Buffalo Bill Cody, and harboring a dislike for Derek Mills that he didn't think was going to go away.

EIGHT

Clint walked to Rush Street, which was only about two blocks from the hotel. When he reached it, though, he discovered that he was far away from the address on the envelope. James Hannigan's office— or home—must have been at the other end of Rush Street. It was a nice day, though, so he decided to walk rather than take a cab.

It turned out to be almost a mile walk, but he got to see a lot of the city that way—a lot of Rush Street, actually, which was largely businesses, restaurants, saloons, and some buildings with offices and residences.

Finally, he reached the building that matched the address. One look at the various shingles hanging on the wall outside was enough to tell him that it housed several different businesses. One of them read JAMES HANNIGAN, INVESTIGATOR. So, Hannigan was a colleague of Talbot Roper. Clint might have guessed that much.

Clint went inside, wondering how many floors the building had, and what floor Hannigan's office was on. When he got inside he found a list on the wall of names and room numbers. Next to Hannigan's name it said "Rm. 201." Clint assumed this meant the man's office was on the second floor and went up the stairs.

In the second floor hall he walked to the front of the building and found the door to Room 201. The lettering on the door was the same as on the front of the building. Clint knocked twice before he realized the door was ajar.

"Hello?" he called out.

No answer.

His knocks had opened the door a few inches. He put his hand against it and pushed it open the rest of the way.

"Anyone here?"

Clint found himself in an outer office, with an empty desk. He was about to look around when he smelled something. He sniffed air and realized that it was an odor he had smelled many times before.

Blood, and a lot of it.

He moved quickly to the open door that had to lead into Hannigan's office. When he entered, the smell hit him even harder. He saw the blood on the desk first, and then the man on the floor behind it. The blood had spread out around the man, almost like a halo around the body. Clint didn't know how much blood the human body held, but the dead man looked as if he had lost most of the blood in his body.

Clint moved just a bit closer, close enough to see that the man's throat had been cut from ear to ear. He looked around, not knowing what he was looking for, and then noticed the floor. There was a set of bloody footprints leading from the body to the door. He hadn't noticed them when he first walked in, but he followed them now, and they went to the door of the office and stopped there. In a corner he saw a crumpled newspaper with blood on it. He assumed that the killer had paused there to wipe the blood off his shoes or boots with the paper before stepping out into the hall. Apparently he hadn't cared about the tracks he'd left behind in both the inner and outer office.

Clint didn't know who the dead man was, but it was probably a safe assumption that it was James Hannigan. He paused to consider his options, and decided he had two. The first was to go and find a policeman and report what had happened. The second was to get out of there and forget about it, not get involved—but he was already involved. Roper had asked him to stop there, and he couldn't very well tell Roper that he'd found his friend dead and had done nothing about it. There would be no way to justify that sort of action.

He touched the pocket that held the envelope Roper had given him to deliver to Hannigan. Even if he reported this to the police, what would he tell them about his being there? Would Roper want him to tell?

He finally made up his mind about what to do, and left to find a telegraph office.

When Clint came out the front door of the building, he almost ran into a man who was passing by.

"Oh, sorry," he said, barely giving the man a look.

He hurried down the street and did not see the man looking after him. Nor did he see the man go into the small hotel a few doors down from the building where James Hannigan's office was.

NINE

Clint found a telegraph office a few blocks away, on Michigan Avenue. He went inside, pulled Talbot Roper's address from the recesses of his brain, and then tried to compose a telegram telling the man that James Hannigan was dead. He didn't know quite how to do it, not knowing if Roper and Hannigan were actually friends or just colleagues. He finally decided to simply take the straightforward approach. He wrote:

> HANNIGAN EXPIRED BEFORE DELIVERY.
> WIRE INSTRUCTIONS.
>   CLINT ADAMS

Well, it wasn't so straightforward, but he thought Roper would understand.

"Where can I find you for the answer?" the clerk asked.

"Right here," Clint said, realizing that he was a

little breathless. "I'll wait for it right here."

"It might take a while."

"As soon as he gets the wire," Clint said, "he'll send an answer."

"Might take them a while on the other end to find him," the clerk said.

"The faster you send it," Clint said testily, "the quicker they can get started."

"Okay," the clerk said, "but you don't have to bite my head off."

Clint decided not to apologize to the man. He was, after all, annoying.

There was a bench against one wall and Clint sat on it. He touched the letter in his pocket once again, but did not take it out. There was no guarantee that it had anything to do with Hannigan's murder. He'd just leave it where it was until he heard from Roper.

He had time sitting there to think about Buffalo Bill Cody's offers, and he did so to try to keep his mind off the sight of James Hannigan lying on the floor with his throat viciously cut. The killer must have been a strong man to cut Hannigan's throat in that way. Clint had the feeling that if he had moved the body the head might have . . .

Cody's offers, both of them, were intriguing. By far the most intriguing was the opportunity to hunt with the man. Clint had heard from Wyatt Earp what a great buffalo hunter Cody had been. It would be interesting to watch the man hunt, even though there were no more buffalo to hunt.

It also would have been interesting to see Cody's Wild West Show. Clint had heard that it was quite a spectacle, but he'd never had the opportunity to see it himself.

As much as he tried not to, his mind kept going back to James Hannigan's office. The footprints on the floor would certainly help to indicate the size of his killer. He tried to conjure them up and look at them again, but the thing he kept seeing over and over again was Hannigan's cut throat . . .

Clint had seen plenty of death, and had indeed cut a throat or two himself when the need arose, but he had never seen a cut this vicious—and he had seen throats cut by Apaches. When an Apache cut a white man's throat, however, there was never anything personal in it. Clint had the feeling that whoever had killed James Hannigan in that way had something *very* personal against the man.

"Mister?"

Clint jerked his head up and looked at the clerk. From the expression on the man's face, he had called his name several times before getting his attention.

"Thought maybe you dozed off," the man said as Clint came up to the counter, "or maybe died."

"I'm alive," Clint said. "Did the reply come?"

"Yep," the man said, "just like you said, quick as spit."

Clint waited a moment, then said, "Can I have it?"

"Oh, yeah," the man said, "here."

Clint took the telegram to the bench and read it while sitting there. It read:

GO TO POLICE. PLAY IT STRAIGHT. HOLD LETTER
FOR ME. TAKING FIRST TRAIN. THANKS.

TAL ROPER

Clint folded the telegram and put it into the same pocket with the letter. He went back up to the counter.

"Another telegram?" the clerk asked.

"No," Clint said. "Where is the nearest place I can find a policeman?"

"Was the service that bad?"

Clint just stared. As far as he was concerned, this man was not funny.

"There's a police station two blocks north and one block east. You can't miss it."

"Thanks."

"You ain't from around here, are you?"

"No."

"I could tell."

Clint left and started walking north, going over in his head what he was going to tell the police. Roper's telegram had said to play it straight. Did that mean telling them Roper's name?

In Talbot Roper's business, the word "straight" had a totally different meaning than in the rest of society.

TEN

It took Clint a long time to get a policeman to go back to Hannigan's office with him, and when he finally did, it was a uniformed patrolman.

"Don't you think we should have somebody a little higher up the ladder?" he asked.

The uniformed man looked at him. He was a young man, probably in his late twenties, with a very serious expression on his face at all times. He said his name was "Officer Tillis."

"First I'll take a look at the scene, sir," Tillis said. "If I think it warrants someone in higher authority, I'll send for someone."

"Oh," Clint said, "I think you can be sure it will require someone."

Tillis said, "I'll be the judge of that."

When they walked into Hannigan's office, Tillis wrinkled his nose, but Clint took him into the inner office without a word. The young man took one look at Hannigan's body and vomited down the front of his coat and pants and onto his shoes.

Clint knew he was being cruel, but he couldn't help himself. He asked, "Think this calls for someone in more authority?"

The next time Clint walked into Hannigan's office it was in the company of Sergeant Folkes and Lieutenant O'Grady.

Folkes was a squat, barrel-chested man in his forties with the red-lined nose and cheeks of a heavy drinker.

O'Grady, on the other hand, was tall, slender, clear of skin and eyes. He was about ten years younger than the sergeant.

"Is this the way you found him, Mr. Adams?" the lieutenant asked.

"Just like that."

Folkes leaned over Hannigan, carefully avoiding the puddle left behind by Officer Tillis, and studied him for a moment. "He's dead."

"I told you that."

"If you don't mind, Mr. Adams," O'Grady said, "we'd just like you to answer our questions."

"Go ahead and ask."

Instead, O'Grady looked at Folkes.

"Somebody didn't like him," Folkes said, still examining the body. "They almost cut his head off."

"A strong man, then," O'Grady said.

"I'd say," Folkes agreed.

O'Grady looked at Clint.

"Did you know Mr. Hannigan?"

"No," Clint said. "I didn't even know if it was Hannigan."

"It is," O'Grady said. "We know Mr. Hannigan, don't we, Sergeant?"

Folkes nodded.

"Always knew he'd end up like this, too."

"Why?" Clint asked, but neither of the men answered.

"If you didn't know him, what were you doing here?" O'Grady asked.

Clint had already decided how to answer this question.

"I was just looking him up on the advice of a friend," he said.

"Who's the friend?"

"A man named Talbot Roper, from Denver."

O'Grady and Folkes exchanged a look.

"Do you know Roper?"

"We've heard of him," O'Grady said.

"He and Hannigan were in the same business," Folkes said.

"Only we hear Roper is not as sleazy," O'Grady said.

"But maybe not by much, huh?" Folkes added.

Clint wondered if this was a well-polished act that these two put on regularly.

"How well do you know Roper?" O'Grady asked.

"Very well," Clint said. "We're old friends."

"Why did he tell you to look up Hannigan?"

"To say hello."

"Just to say hello?" O'Grady asked.

"That's right."

"Does Roper know about this yet?" the lieutenant asked.

Clint hesitated just a moment—a moment during which he admitted to himself that Lieutenant

O'Grady was very good at his job.

"How could he?" Clint asked.

O'Grady shrugged.

"I thought maybe you took the time to send him a telegram."

"Before talking to you? Why would I do that?"

"I don't know," O'Grady said, "why would you?"

"I wouldn't."

"So you found him like this and came directly to us?" Folkes asked.

"That's right . . . well, it took me a while to find you and then they sent me over with that Officer Tillis. It was only after he finished puking up his lunch that we came to get you."

"You should have asked for us first thing," O'Grady said.

"I did," Clint said. "I asked for someone in authority, but he insisted he had to come and take a look first."

"What's your business in Chicago, Mr. Adams?" Lieutenant O'Grady asked.

"I'm here to see a friend."

"What friend?"

"He has nothing to do with this."

"Are you refusing to give us his name?"

Clint hesitated, then said, "Mark Eaton."

"The newspaperman?" Folkes asked.

Clint nodded.

"I don't read the newspaper all that much," O'Grady said to Folkes.

"He writes for the *Tribune*," Folkes said.

O'Grady nodded, and turned back to Clint.

"Are you from Denver, Mr. Adams?"

"No."

"But you came here from Denver?"

"Yes."

"Where are you from?"

"All over."

"Anywhere specific?"

"No."

"You move around, then."

"Yes."

"A lot?"

"Yes."

"You're becoming a man of few words, Mr. Adams."

"I'm sorry," Clint said, "I thought you were asking me 'yes' and 'no' questions. Did you want me to elaborate on something?"

"Yes," O'Grady said, "but why don't we do that back at the station, hmm?"

ELEVEN

Clint went back to the police station with Lieutenant O'Grady and Sergeant Folkes.

"If you'll have a seat in my office, Mr. Adams, I have to make arrangements for Mr. Hannigan's body to be removed. I won't be long."

"I'd like to get back to my hotel," Clint said. "Couldn't Sergeant Folkes question me?"

"We do that together," Folkes said. "Just have a seat, sir, and we won't be long."

They showed him to O'Grady's office, where he sat in front of the man's empty desk for about twenty minutes before the two policemen returned.

"Sorry it took so long," O'Grady said.

He sat behind the desk while Folkes stood off to one side, out of Clint's peripheral vision. Clint figured this was by design. They had probably taken half the time they were away to figure out how to handle him.

"Where were we?" O'Grady asked.

"You tell me."

"Oh, yes," O'Grady said, "your reason for coming to Chicago."

"He told us that," Folkes said. "Come to see a friend of his."

"Oh, yeah, that's right," the lieutenant said. "A newspaperman?"

"Right," Folkes said, "for the *Trib*. Mark Eaton."

"Right, Eaton. Have you seen your friend yet, Mr. Adams?"

"No," Clint said. "I only arrived this morning."

"Have you seen anyone since your arrival? Talked to anyone?"

"Sure."

"Who?"

"The desk clerk at the hotel? You mean like that? Or somebody like Buffalo Bill Cody?"

O'Grady frowned.

"Let's leave out the clerks and bartenders, why don't we?" O'Grady said. "What's this about Buffalo Bill Cody?"

"I had a drink with him this afternoon."

"The real Cody?" Folkes asked.

Clint turned his head to look at the sergeant for the first time.

"That's right."

"You know him?"

"Yes," Clint said. "I'll be seeing him tomorrow."

Folkes looked at O'Grady. A look passed between them that meant nothing to Clint, so he waited.

"Who else have you seen?"

"A man named Blaylock, who works for Cody; somebody named, uh, Mills. He owns a theater where Cody is going to play. Oh, and a young man named Jerald something or other."

"Derek Mills?" O'Grady asked.

"That's right. You know him?"

"I do."

"Mr. Adams," Folkes said, "can I see the bottom of your boots?"

"Checking for blood, Sergeant? I'm afraid I probably stepped in some while I was in the office. Didn't you?"

"Humor me, please."

The sergeant approached and Clint lifted first one foot and then the other for his inspection.

"Thank you."

"Sure."

Folkes went back to his former position.

"Is there anything else, Lieutenant?" Clint asked.

"Oh, Mr. Adams," O'Grady said, "there's a lot more."

"Am I suspected of something here?"

"Frankly, yes."

"Of what?"

"Well, lying for one."

"About what?"

"Suppose you tell me?"

"Look, I found a body and I reported it to the police. Isn't that what you want citizens to do?"

"Of course."

"And do you treat all law-abiding citizens this way?"

"Of course not."

"Then why me?"

"Because you're lying, Mr. Adams."

"About what?"

O'Grady sat forward and leaned one arm on his

desk. He regarded Clint for several seconds with a baleful stare before speaking.

"I don't know that, Mr. Adams, I just know that you are."

Clint shook his head, but didn't say anything.

"Empty your pockets, please."

"What?"

"I asked that you empty your pockets."

"What for?"

"I'd like to see what you have in them."

"What do you expect me to have in them?"

O'Grady sighed and looked up at the ceiling.

"Mr. Adams, I'm asking you to cooperate with this investigation by emptying your pockets."

"I don't see what the contents of my pockets have to do with anything."

"Empty them!" O'Grady shouted, slamming his hand down on the desk.

Clint was startled by the explosion, but he recovered quickly.

"You're not going to get anywhere, Lieutenant, trying to treat me like a common criminal."

"Oh, I know you're not a common criminal, Mr. Adams." O'Grady said calmly. "In fact, I know exactly who you are."

"Do you?"

"Oh, yes. Your celebrity has spread this far and, I'm sure, even further. We've heard of the Gunsmith, haven't we, Sergeant?"

"Yes, we have."

"Is that why you're giving me a hard time?" Clint asked. "Because I have a reputation?"

"No," O'Grady said, "I'm giving you a hard time because you're lying to me."

"I don't know what I'd be lying about, Lieutenant," Clint said, "but I do know one thing."

"What's that?"

"I'm leaving." He stood up.

"Sit back down, please."

"Either charge me or let me walk out," Clint said.

O'Grady spread his hands.

"I have nothing to charge you with."

"Then I'm leaving."

The two men stared at each other for a few moments, and then O'Grady leaned back.

"I'm going to allow you to leave, Mr. Adams, because you've been through something of an ordeal today—or have you seen this kind of thing before?"

"I've seen dead men before," Clint said, "but nothing quite this . . . vicious."

O'Grady nodded and said, "Okay. Just tell us what hotel you're staying in and you can go."

"I'm at the Drake."

"The Drake," O'Grady said. "Very comfortable."

"May I go now?"

"Of course. We appreciate your cooperation."

As Clint started for the door, O'Grady said, "Oh, one more thing."

"Yes?"

"We'll be calling on you at your hotel, probably tomorrow. I'd like to talk to you about this again, once you've had time to think about it."

"About what?"

"Oh, what you may have seen, any ideas you might have. Who knows? You might remember something important."

"Who knows?" Clint repeated, and left.

TWELVE

Clint left the police station and went right to the Drake hotel. Before going to his room he stopped in the bar for a drink. He needed one.

"A beer, Mr. Adams?" the young bartender asked.

"No," Clint said, "whiskey."

The barman put a shot glass of whiskey in front of him. Clint downed it and said, "Another."

The bartender refilled the glass and asked, "A bad day?"

"You don't know the half of it."

The bartender waited, as if he thought Clint was going to tell him the rest of it.

It was early evening now and the bar was a little busier. A man at the other end of the bar tapped it lightly with his glass and the bartender went to serve him.

Clint turned and surveyed the room. Most of the tables were taken up with men drinking and talking. None of them knew anything about James Hannigan

47

lying on the floor of his office, his throat cut, his head almost severed.

This kind of violence would not have shocked Clint if he had come across it on the trail somewhere in the West. Here in Chicago, though, he'd been totally unprepared for what he had found in James Hannigan's office. He could still smell the man's blood in his nostrils, and wondered how long it would take for the stench to fade.

"Another one?" the bartender asked, returning.

"No, thanks," Clint said.

"How about something to eat? Our steaks are real good. Want one rare?"

Clint closed his eyes. He wasn't ready for a rare steak yet.

"No, thanks."

"What about—" the man started, but Clint simply turned and walked away.

He went back to his room and washed his face and hands. His jacket was on the back of a chair. He went to it now and removed the telegraph message from Roper and the letter he was going to deliver to James Hannigan. If Clint had been forced to empty his pockets in O'Grady's office, the lieutenant would have known that he had lied about contacting Talbot Roper about the murder. Why he had lied he wasn't sure, since Roper's telegram told him to play it straight. He knew nothing about the contents of the letter, so why was he so reluctant to let O'Grady see it, or even to open it himself?

He stared at it now, wondering if he should open it. No, Roper's telegram had also said that he'd be arriving in Chicago as soon as possible. He could wait for the man to arrive to find out—if Roper would even tell him. If not—well, it was never any of his business in the first place, was it?

He didn't think the police seriously considered him a suspect, so his part in Hannigan's murder was finished. He'd found the body and reported it. There was no reason for him to be involved at all anymore, and that was what he was going to tell Lieutenant O'Grady the next time he saw him. He wanted no part of this.

No part.

When Clint woke it was barely two. He'd decided to lie down on the bed for a moment, and that was almost six hours ago. He couldn't believe he'd slept that long, and now it was two o'clock in the morning and what was he going to do? He couldn't very well go back to sleep. For one thing, he was hungry and for another, he'd never get to sleep after a six hour "nap."

He decided to get dressed and go downstairs to see what the hotel—or Chicago—had to offer him at two in the morning.

THIRTEEN

When he reached the lobby, it was still. After all, it was two a.m. He did hear some noise from the bar, however, and walked over to look inside. He was surprised to see a group of men sitting at one of the tables. One of the group saw him looking in and walked over. It was the bartender who had served him, the one who had the dime novel about him.

"Bar's closed, Mr. Adams," the man said.

"What about them?" Clint asked, pointing.

"Oh," the bartender said, "that's just a bunch of guys who work here. After they go off their shift sometimes we sit around and drink, or play poker."

"Which is it tonight? Clint asked.

"Well," the man said, "we been drinking, but we-'re kind of split on poker. Four of us want to, and four of us don't want to. Can't get a good game going with just four people. Well, you know that."

"That means you need a fifth."

"Well . . . yeah, if we want to play. Why? Are you

looking for something to do at two in the morning?"

"Yup."

The man smiled. The prospect of playing poker with Clint seemed to excite him.

"Wait, wait," he said, "I'll go and tell them."

Clint waited in the doorway while the bartender went over to talk to the others. As he watched he saw all of them—not just four, but all—shake their heads. When the bartender returned, he had a glum look on his face.

"I'm afraid they don't want to play poker with you, Mr. Adams."

"Why not?"

"Well . . . they're afraid of you."

"Why is that?"

"Uh, well, I told them who you are."

"They don't think I'm going to shoot them if they win my money, do they?"

"No, no," the man said, "just the opposite. They think you're gonna win all their money."

"Oh, I see."

The men at the table stood up and filed out of the bar, saying good night to the bartender and giving Clint wary looks. He heard them all call the bartender Tom.

"Well, Tom, what are you going to do with yourself this morning?"

"I don't know," Tom said, scratching his head. "To tell you the truth, I ain't really sleepy."

"Do you know of someplace else to go to get a drink? And maybe a poker game? Someplace that doesn't close this early?"

"Well . . . I know a couple of places . . ."

"I'll buy the drinks," Clint said.

Tom grinned and said, "Okay, let's go."

On the way out of the hotel Clint found out that Tom's last name was Davis, and that he was twenty-five years old.

"You look younger."

"Even with these?" Tom asked, pointing to the muttonchops.

"Uh, yes, even with those. Is that why you grew those? To look older?"

"Well, yes."

"Why?"

"Women," Tom said frankly. "They like older men."

"Go after younger women," Clint suggested, "ones who will consider you an older man."

Tom shook his head.

"You don't understand," he said. "This is a high-class hotel. The women who stay here are older."

"How much older?"

"Thirties, usually."

"Why is that?"

"It's expensive," Tom said. "If they have the money to stay here themselves, then they're older. If they're young women, then they're being kept by someone."

"I see. Well, why not grow a beard?"

Tom touched his chin, which was surpisingly smooth.

"I've tried, but it won't grow in. Just the mustache and the muttonchops."

"I have a suggestion, Tom."

"What?"

"Get rid of the muttonchops. Keep the mustache if you like, but get rid of the rest. It doesn't look good on you."

The younger man didn't take offense.

"I guess you're right," he said. "It wasn't really working anyway."

"No women?"

Tom shrugged.

"I don't really have that much luck with women."

Clint decided to help the young man.

"Which way do we go?" he asked.

"That way," Tom said, pointing.

"Are we walking?"

"Yes. It's not far."

"Let's go, then," Clint said, putting his arm around the young man's shoulders, "and I'll tell you a little something about women . . ."

FOURTEEN

The place Tom Davis had in mind was just four blocks away from the Drake, on Rush Street. Actually, it was in an alley off of Rush Street. They had to go down the alley, down a flight of concrete steps to a solid metal door. Tom knocked and a small slot opened. They were examined by a pair of cold, brown eyes.

"Come on, Leo," Tom said.

"Who's that?" a voice asked.

"Just a friend. He's looking for a drink, and maybe one round of poker."

"You vouch for him?"

"Of course."

The slot closed and there was the sound of several locks being disengaged. The door opened and a man who was almost as wide as he was tall stared at them.

"He's your responsibility, Tom."

"Leo, don't worry, he's . . . okay."

On the way over Clint had instructed Tom not to

tell anyone his name. He'd felt the younger man was about to slip, and was happy to see him recover in time.

"Okay, then," Leo said, "come on in."

Tom looked at Clint and said, "Come on." Clint followed him in.

The interior was smoky, and it had everything that the bar at the Drake did not, and everything that a saloon in the West did. There were gaming tables of all kinds, and women in brightly colored dresses, many of them low-cut, walking around, tickling men under the chin or sitting in their laps.

"Is this what you had in mind?" Tom asked.

Clint nodded.

"Come on, I'll buy you a drink," Clint said.

They went to the bar where the bartender, a man in his early thirties with a two-day growth of beard on his chin, greeted Tom by name.

"What'll ya have?"

"A beer," Clint said.

"Me, too," Tom said.

Clint didn't know just how thrilled Tom was to be drinking with the Gunsmith. He'd read everything he could about Clint Adams, and he couldn't believe the kind of day he'd had, meeting both Clint Adams and Buffalo Bill Cody.

"So, what did you and Colonel Cody talk about today?" Tom asked when they had their beers.

"You really want to know?"

"Sure I do."

"He offered me a job."

Tom's eyes widened.

"With his Wild West Show?"

"That's right."

"Wow . . . are you gonna take it?"

"No."

"Why not?"

"Because I don't like being on display, Tom. I never have."

"But . . . your reputation . . ."

"What about it?"

"Well, it's—I mean, isn't that like being on display? Having a reputation?"

"At this point in time, Tom, there's not much I can do about the fact that I have a reputation," Clint explained. "I can, however, keep from putting myself on further display."

"But, wouldn't he be paying you a lot of money?"

"I don't know," Clint said. "I didn't ask. Besides, I don't need a lot of money."

"I thought everybody needed a lot of money."

"Maybe in the city," Clint said, "but not out west."

Clint held his beer and looked around. He didn't like what he saw. This was too much a gambling establishment, which meant that most of the people gambling here were rather desperate about it. He didn't like to play cards with desperate people. It was just as well that there was not a poker game going on. There seemed to be more blackjack, faro, and roulette than anything else, and none of those games appealed to him.

"You want to play something?" Tom asked.

"No, but you go ahead. I'll just watch for a while."

"I thought you wanted to gamble?"

"I like poker, Tom. None of these other games appeal to me. But you go ahead. I'll watch."

"Well, all right. I'm going to play some roulette."

To Clint's way of thinking, roulette took no skill. You played a number and hoped that it came up. At least with cards—poker, blackjack, faro—there were some decisions that had to be made, some odds to be figured. Roulette was just watching a stupid little ball go round and round until the wheel stopped and the ball landed on one of the numbers. He'd played it before, when he just had some time to kill, but it was not something he liked to do.

He worked on his beer and watched the people. A tall black-haired woman caught his eye. She was sitting at a blackjack table, and didn't seem to be in the company of anyone. He was seeing her in profile, and it was a profile he liked. She had a straight nose, a nice chin, was mostly slender, but still exhibited an attractive thrust of breast. Her arms and shoulders were bare, and her skin was pale and smooth.

He continued to watch her as first one man and then a second sat next to her and tried to engage her in conversation. Both were rebuffed, and were not happy about it. Clint noticed later that both men ended up standing at the bar together. He supposed that they were friends, and probably the same type—a type that she apparently did not care for.

The longer he watched, the more convinced he became that she was alone. He would have liked to talk to her, but he suspected that one reason she had sent the other two men packing was that she didn't like to talk when she was playing. She concentrated very hard on her game, and from what he could see she was winning.

He was working on a second beer when Tom reappeared.

"How did you do?" Clint asked.

"Not well."

"Want another beer?"

"I need one."

Clint waved at the bartender, and the man brought a beer for Tom.

"Do you come here often?" Clint asked.

"A few times a week. Why?"

"Do you know that woman?" Clint gestured with his free hand.

"Oh, yeah—I mean, no. I mean, I've seen her here before, but I don't know who she is."

"Never tried talking to her?"

"Me? Talk to her? She's way out of my league, Clint."

"How do you know that?"

"Just look at her. She's gorgeous. She needs a man who can spend money on her."

Clint looked at Tom and said, "If you shaved some of that hair off your face she might like you."

"I look nineteen without this hair."

"Maybe she likes younger men."

"I don't think so," Tom said, sipping his beer. "What about you? Why don't you talk to her?"

"Oh, I will, but not while she's gambling. She's very serious about her gambling—or blackjack, anyway. I haven't seen her play anything else."

"Neither have I. Every time I've seen her she's been playing blackjack."

"Well," Clint said, "I'll just watch awhile longer and see what happens."

"I'm gonna finish this beer and then try the wheel again."

"Why don't you play something else?"

"No, I like roulette."

"Why?"

"Because when I gamble I don't like to think."

Clint didn't say anything, but not thinking while you gambled sounded to him like a good way to make gambling harder—and it generally didn't need the help.

FIFTEEN

Tom went off and tried his hand at roulette again, with much the same result.

Clint remained at the bar, watching the woman play. At one point he asked the bartender, a burly man in his forties, if he knew her name.

"Nope," the man said. "We get lots of people in and out of here, mister."

"I thought she was a regular."

"There's lots of regulars in here whose names I don't know. I tend bar and mind my own business."

"That's probably a good way to do it," Clint said.

The man nodded his head and went off to do it some more.

Clint noticed that the two men the woman had rejected were also continuing to watch her. They did so with their heads together, like coconspirators who were planning something. Finally, the woman got up from the table and cashed in her chips. Clint decided not to approach her, but to watch what happened when she left.

After she finished cashing in her chips, she put her money away in her purse, and did not stop at the bar for a drink. She started for the door, and Clint watched as the two men moved away from the bar to follow her.

Clint hurried over to the roulette table and said to Tom, "Come on."

"Wait," Tom said, "the wheel—"

"Come on!"

"I have a dollar on the table."

"I'll give you two dollars," Clint said, pulling on the younger man's arm. "Come on!"

"All right," Tom said, allowing himself to be pulled toward the door. "What's going on?"

"We're going to help a lady."

"What lady?"

"The one who was playing blackjack."

"Did you talk to her?"

"No."

"Then how do you know she needs help?"

They went outside and up the stairs. There was no one in sight, but there was only one way in and out of the alley. Clint rushed ahead with Tom trailing just behind.

"What's going on?" he asked.

"Two men are going to rob that woman."

"How do you know that?"

"Because I've been watching them."

"I thought you were watching the woman."

"I've been watching the woman and the two men."

"How come—"

"Quiet!"

They came to the mouth of the alley and out onto

Rush Street. Clint looked both ways but didn't see anyone.

"They couldn't have gotten far," he said. "They must have turned a corner." But which one?

"I watched her go that way one night," Tom said.

Clint looked at him.

"Hey, she's pretty, and we left at the same time. She went that way." He pointed to the right.

"Let's go," Clint said.

They turned right and hurried down the block. Clint figured when they got to the corner they were going to have to pick a direction again, but before they got there he heard something.

"Wait!"

They stopped and stood still while he continued to listen. The sound came again. Scuffling, the sound of someone groaning, or grunting . . . the sound of a struggle.

"Is there another alley?" he asked.

"We passed one," Tom said, "a small one."

"Show me."

They retraced their steps and as they did the sounds got louder. Sure enough, when they reached the smaller, narrower alley they could see the silhouettes of three people struggling.

"Hold her still," one man said.

"I wanna touch her tits."

"Let's just get the money."

"I wanna touch her," the other man complained.

"Come on," Clint said.

He rushed into the alley, not sure whether or not Tom was behind him. It didn't matter, though. He was going to help the woman with or without the young bartender's help.

SIXTEEN

As Clint got closer he was able to see better. One man had the woman from behind, one arm pinning her arms to her sides and the other hand over her mouth, while the other man was grabbing at her in front. Apparently, it was the man in front who wanted to touch her. He had torn the front of her gown so that her breasts were exposed. His hands were on her, clutching at her. In a split second Clint saw that the look in her eyes was not one of fear, but of anger. He liked her for that.

He grabbed the man who was touching her and spun him around.

"Wha—" the man said, but his words were cut off by Clint's fist in his face. The man's nose exploded in a gusher of blood as he staggered back.

"Hey!" the man holding the woman said. At that point she stomped on his instep with the heel of her boot. He shouted and released her. As she ducked away, Clint stepped in and hit the man in the stomach. Before he could follow up, the woman got between him and the man and punched her assailant full in the face. The man's head snapped back and slammed into the brick wall behind him. He slumped to the ground, but she wasn't finished with him yet. She kicked him twice, once in the ribs and once in the head. She turned then to the other man, who was still on his feet, but effectively helpless. He was holding his hands over his face, trying to stem the tide of blood. She took two steps and then kicked him right between the legs. The man opened his mouth to cry out but nothing came out. He grabbed his crotch, staggered back, and then fell on his butt.

"Bastard!" she shouted.

She took a step, with intentions of kicking him again, but Clint stepped in and grabbed her arm to stop her.

She whirled on him, drawing her fist back.

"Hey, hold it!" he shouted. "I'm the guy who helped you, remember?"

Her eyes were blazing and for a moment he didn't think he was getting through to her. Slowly, the fire went out and she really looked at him for the first time.

"Are you all right?" he asked.

"Yes," she said, "I—I think so." She looked down then and said, "My purse."

"Here it is," Tom said. He stepped forward and held it out to her. She looked at him warily.

"It's okay," Clint said. "He's with me."

She hesitated, then nodded and accepted her bag.

"Is everything there?" Clint asked.

"I'm sure it is," she said. "They didn't have time."

Suddenly she became aware that Tom was staring

at her. She looked down at her naked breasts and said, "Oh."

She gathered the tattered remnants of her gown and tried to cover herself.

"Here." Clint took off his jacket and draped it around her shoulders. She pulled the front closed to cover herself.

"Thank you."

"Let's get out of here," Clint suggested.

"A-all right."

The three of them walked out of the alley onto Rush Street.

"Do you want to send for the police?" Clint asked her.

"No," she said immediately, "I—I just want to go home."

"All right," Clint said. "I'll take you."

"It's not far."

"Fine, I'll walk you."

"Really," she said, "I can find my own way."

He smiled and said, "I'll need my jacket back."

"Oh," she said, laughing uncomfortably. "Well, a-all right . . ."

Clint turned to Tom and said, "I'll see you tomorrow."

"What?" Tom said. Then he said, "Oh, I get it." He got what he probably thought was a knowing look on his face. "Okay, see you tomorrow."

Clint looked at the woman and asked, "Which way?"

She hesitated, then said, "This way."

SEVENTEEN

"There's something I should tell you," she said.

"Like your name?"

"Oh," she said, "it's Pamela Lutz—uh, Pam, since you probably saved my life."

"I think they were probably just after your money," Clint said.

"And rape," she said.

"Uh, yes, that, too."

"Where did you come from?"

"I was in the, uh, gambling establishment where you were playing blackjack."

She turned her head to look at him more carefully.

"Oh," she said, "you were watching me from the bar."

He smiled and said, "Guilty. They were watching you, too, but they had something else in mind for you."

"Really?" she asked. "And what did you have in mind for me?"

"Well . . . not the same thing, I can assure you."

"I guess not."

"I saw them follow you when you left and assumed the worst."

"I'm lucky you assumed correctly, Mr. . . . ."

"Adams, Clint Adams."

"Clint," she said, "since at the least you saved my money and my virtue."

"It was my pleasure."

"My home is on the next block," she said, "but there's something I should tell you before we get there."

"What's that?"

"I'm Mrs. Pamela Lutz."

"Ah, there's a husband."

"Yes, and he'll probably be waiting up."

"And?"

"And he'll be angry."

"I don't blame him."

"No, not because of what happened," she said. "Because of the gambling."

"Oh."

"He might make a scene," she said, "but when he hears the whole story I'm sure he'll want to thank you."

"Are you saying you want me to go inside with you?"

"I—I think so. I think that would be best."

Clint wondered what had changed her mind. Initially she had not wanted him to walk her home at all. Now she wanted him to go inside. He wondered if she assumed her husband's anger would not be displayed as freely in front of a stranger.

"All right," he said, "I'll come inside."

She seemed to breathe a sigh of relief.

"Thank you."

They walked the last block and then came to a two-story brick house. As they mounted the steps she took her key from her bag, but before she could fit it into the lock the door opened.

"Pamela, goddamn it! Where the hell have you been?" He saw Clint then and demanded, "Who the hell are you?"

"Philip," she said, "can we talk inside?"

He gave her an annoyed look, Clint a curious one, then backed up and said, "Come in, then. Come in."

She stepped inside and Clint followed. They were in an entry hall, which was well lit by two lamps. Philip Lutz saw his wife wearing Clint's jacket.

"Is that his? Take it off."

She opened her mouth to say something, then closed it, shrugged, and took off the jacket, handing it to Clint. Philip Lutz's mouth fell open when he saw his wife's naked breasts. He hadn't even noticed that she had a bruise on her cheek.

"What's the meaning of this? Cover yourself up!"

"Make up your mind, Philip," she said.

"Is this your doing?" the man demanded of Clint. "I'll call the police—"

"Philip, if you'll let me explain—"

"Go ahead, go ahead," he said, cutting her off. "Explain—but for Christ's sake put something on."

Clint gave her the jacket back, and she donned it.

"You went gambling, didn't you?"

"Yes, I did," she said, "and I won ten thousand dollars."

"And does that make up for the fifty thousand you lost last week? And the twenty the week before?"

"Philip—"

"Never mind. What the hell happened to you? Why are you so . . . disheveled?

"I'm disheveled, as you put it, because two men tried to rob and rape me. They would have succeeded if not for this man. He saved me."

Philip Lutz looked at Clint, still scowling.

"Is that true?" he asked.

"Well . . . yes," Clint said, wondering why the man would doubt such a story coming from his wife.

In the light Clint was able to see that Pamela Lutz was at least twenty years younger than her husband, who looked to be in his mid-fifties. He had gray hair that was white at the temples, and the skin of his neck was loose and wrinkled. He was once a tall man, but now his shoulders had a slump to them. He was not aging well. His wife, on the other hand, in her mid-thirties, was aging quite gracefully. She was older than Clint had first deduced in the dimly lit casino, but what he saw now was only an improvement.

"I'm grateful to you, Mr. . . . . "

"His name is Clint Adams."

"Mr. Adams. I thank you for saving my wife and bringing her home safely."

"It was nothing," Clint said. "I was passing by—"

"It's late, Pamela," the man said, ignoring Clint. "You should get cleaned up and get to bed. You've been through an ordeal."

"Yes," she said, "I have. If you'll get me something else to wear, Philip, we can return Mr. Adams's jacket and he can be on his way."

"Yes, yes, of course. I'll go and get you something."

He started to leave, then stopped and turned to

look at them. Did he think they were going to do something in his absence? Finally he left and Clint heard the sounds of him going up a flight of steps.

He turned to Pamela Lutz and found her staring at him strangely.

EIGHTEEN

Clint couldn't help but notice that she wasn't holding his jacket closed any longer. Her breasts were larger than he might have expected. The flesh was as smooth and pale as marble, and he could see that her nipples were dark brown, with very wide aureola.

"I don't know how to thank you," she said.

"It's not necessary."

"I've never seen you in the club before."

"I've never been there before," he said. "I only arrived in Chicago this morning."

"I see. Will you, uh, be going there again?"

"I don't know," Clint said. "Surely you won't."

"There or a place like it."

"I assume your husband doesn't approve of your gambling?"

"You assume correctly," she said, "but that doesn't stop me. I think we'll see each other again, Clint Adams."

Before he could reply, she reached up and pulled his head down so she could kiss him. His jacket fell from her shoulders and her breasts were crushed against his chest. Her mouth was hot, her tongue darting, and her flesh burned through his shirt.

She had just retrieved the jacket when her husband came walking in. He eyed them suspiciously and handed his wife a dressing gown.

"Thank you, Philip."

She took off Clint's jacket and handed it to him, unmindful of her naked breasts. It was clear that Philip Lutz did not like him ogling his wife's breasts, but Clint thought the man was lucky he hadn't walked in a few moments sooner.

Pamela pulled on the dressing gown, then turned to Clint.

"Thank you very much, Clint. Is there some way we can repay you?"

"I don't think so."

"Perhaps dinner one night? How long will you be in town?"

"I'm not sure—"

"It's late, Pamela. We must allow Mr. Adams to go back to his hotel."

"Where are you staying?" she asked.

"The Drake," he said. "Your husband's right. I better be going."

Both Pamela and Philip walked him to the door and watched him go down the steps. When he got to the bottom, the door closed and he stood there a moment. Sure enough, he heard raised voices from inside. He had the feeling that raising their voices to each other was not a rare occurrence with the Lutzes.

As he walked away, Clint couldn't help but wonder how a man like Philip Lutz expected to satisfy a young, beautiful wife who had the kind of, uh, appetites Pamela Lutz obviously had. He didn't know how long they had been married, but wondered how much longer they would be.

He could still feel Pam Lutz's breasts against his chest, still taste her lips on his, her tongue in his mouth. From the look on her face when she said they would see each other again he didn't doubt it. She had, after all, asked him what hotel he was staying at.

The last thing Clint needed—in addition to everything that had happened since he arrived in Chicago—was to get involved with a married woman—especially an unhappy, unfulfilled married woman who apparently had a strong will of her own.

He could smell her on his jacket, though, and there was still the taste of her there. . . .

Clint decided that in the morning he'd ask Tom if he knew who Philip Lutz was. From the figures the man had been throwing around—twenty thousand dollars, *fifty* thousand dollars—it was plain that he was rich, and rich men were often powerful men.

Before Clint did anything about Pam Lutz, he wanted to know just how powerful.

NINETEEN

When Clint woke the next morning, he couldn't help but pick up his jacket and smell it. Pam Lutz's perfume was still there. He thought back to the night before, to the angry look in her eyes rather than a fearful one. To the way she handled those two men once Clint had gotten her free of them. She was quite a woman.

He went downstairs and had breakfast in the hotel dining room. His next move today was to finally get to see his friend, Mark Eaton. After all, that was the reason he had really come to Chicago.

He was working on his second pot of coffee when he saw Lieutenant O'Grady walk in and look around. He knew even before the man started across the floor to him that it was he the man was looking for.

"Good morning, Mr. Adams."

"Lieutenant."

"May I sit down?"

"Of course. Would you like a cup of coffee?"

74

"Actually, I would. Thank you."

There was another cup on the table, upside down. The lieutenant righted it, and Clint filled it. The man drank his coffee black with no sugar, so he couldn't have been all bad.

"What can I do for you this morning, Lieutenant?" Clint asked.

"Well, actually, I'd just like to see if there was anything else you could remember about yesterday."

"As a matter of fact, there is."

"What?"

"I bumped into a man as I was leaving the building."

"Can you describe him?"

"Not really," Clint said. "I'm a little embarrassed to say I didn't get a real good look at him. I was still kind of shocked at what I'd found."

"That's not the kind of admission I'd expect from a man of your reputation."

"The problem with reputations is that they're real easy to make up, and real hard to live up to."

"I understand that. Do you have any reason to believe this man might have been, say, running from the scene?"

"Well, he wasn't running. I really don't have any reason to think he was involved, it was just something else I remembered. I'm just trying to be helpful."

"I see. Well, I appreciate it."

That seemed to be the end of the conversation, but the man did not get up to leave.

"Was there something else?"

"Actually, there was, yes. I was instructed by my superior to come and see you this morning."

"About the murder?"

"No, about an incident that took place last night," he said, "with Mrs. Philip Lutz?"

Clint sat back, surprised.

"How did you hear about that?"

"Apparently Mr. Lutz wanted to know something about you, so he got in touch with our mayor, who then got in touch with our police commissioner, who passed it down to my captain, who passed it on to me."

Clint raised his eyebrows.

"All of that just this morning?"

"There's been a lot of running around going on, yes."

"So what do you want to ask me about last night?"

"It's fairly well-known that Pamela Lutz enjoys, uh, a variety of vices."

"Including?"

"Gambling," O'Grady said, "and, uh, men."

"Her husband knows about both of these vices?"

"He does," O'Grady said, "although he only admits to one."

"The gambling."

"Yes."

"It figures he wouldn't want to admit to the other. It also explains why he was giving me all kinds of hard looks last night."

"You want to tell me what happened, so I can pass it on?"

"Lutz didn't say?"

"If he did, it got lost in all of the running around."

Clint explained the situation to O'Grady without mentioning the place where they had been.

"Seems like you saved her a lot of trouble."

"I thought so at the time."

"Change your mind?"

"No, but seeing the way she handled those guys after I stepped in, and considering that she wasn't scared, and they weren't armed, maybe she wasn't in as much trouble as I thought."

"What are you suggesting?"

"I'm not suggesting anything."

"You think this was a game she was playing?" O'Grady asked. "Maybe she knew the men?"

"I don't know what kinds of games the lady plays, Lieutenant," Clint said. "As for whether or not she knew the guys, only she knows that."

"Why wasn't the incident reported to the police?" O'Grady asked.

"She didn't want to do that."

O'Grady didn't say anything.

"That might support a theory that she knew them, is that what you're thinking?" Clint asked.

"I'm not sure what I'm thinking."

Clint frowned. Had he stepped into some kind of rough sex game between Pamela Lutz and the two men? If so, it had gotten very rough for them—probably rougher than they had planned on.

O'Grady finished his coffee and stood up.

"Anything else I can do for you, Lieutenant?"

"No," O'Grady said, "just let me know if you think of anything else." Abruptly, the man put out his hand. "The name is Sean, by the way. Sean O'Grady."

He shook the man's hand. As Clint was about to release it, O'Grady gripped his tighter.

"By the way, have you notified your friend yet about what happened?"

"My friend?"

O'Grady released his hand.

"Talbot Roper."

"Oh, yes, I sent him a telegram."

"What's he going to do?"

"I don't know. He didn't confide in me."

O'Grady nodded.

"All right, then. Thanks for the coffee."

"My pleasure."

Clint watched the lieutenant leave the dining room. He wouldn't have to ask Tom Davis about Philip Lutz now. The man was powerful enough to call the mayor of Chicago early in the morning and get immediate results.

That was rich.

TWENTY

Clint and Mark Eaton had agreed to meet for lunch the day after Clint arrived. This was to give Clint time to get settled. He couldn't help but think if he and Eaton had met that first day, he might not have been the one to find James Hannigan's body. He also might not have met Pamela Lutz and her rich and powerful husband, Philip. Clint was quite sure that he was not on Philip Lutz's list of favorite people.

Then again, had he met with Eaton immediately upon his arrival he might not have gotten the chance to meet Buffalo Bill Cody.

Clint spent the morning in his room. He felt that was the best way to avoid trouble. At noon he went down to the dining room, where he was to meet Eaton. Seated at a table with a pot of coffee, he was wondering idly when Talbot Roper would arrive when Eaton walked into the room. He had also been wondering about the envelope Roper had given him. It was still in his pocket, and once or twice he had almost opened it, but had resisted. Eaton's appearance took his mind off of it.

Clint had met Eaton several years ago when the reporter had gone out west for *The Chicago Tribune* and done a series of "on the trail" articles. Clint had convinced Eaton not to write anything about him, and the man—upon his return to Chicago—had complied. He thought that the invitation to Chicago was probably so Eaton could try once again to convince Clint to let him write about him. To Clint, a trip to Chicago had simply sounded good, and he'd accepted. He had no doubt that if Eaton asked and he said no, that would be the end of it. After that— according to his original plan—he would have just gone on to enjoy the city.

That was before dead bodies, rich runaround wives, and job offers from living legends.

Chicago was turning out to be much more than he had bargained for.

Mark Eaton was a tall man with a youthful appearance. In his thirties, he could have passed for a decade younger. The difference between Tom Davis and Eaton was that the reporter enjoyed being taken for a younger man. No muttonchops for him. He was clean-shaven and smelling of bay rum.

As the reporter neared the table, Clint stood up.

"You've been busy," Eaton said, shaking his hand.

"What do you mean?"

"I've heard all about your escapades."

They sat down.

"What escapades?"

"You and Pamela Lutz? You and James Hannigan?"

"Jesus, news travels fast in the city, doesn't it?" Clint asked, surprised.

"It does when you work for a paper like the *Trib*," Eaton said. "My publisher got a message from Philip Lutz. He wanted whatever information we had on you in our morgue files."

"And?"

"We sent him what we had, but if you hadn't convinced me not to write about you three years ago, when we met, there'd be a lot more. Come on, tell poppa all about it. What happened?"

Clint gave Eaton the same version of the Pam Lutz story that he'd given Lieutenant O'Grady.

"Okay, that's what you told the police," Eaton said when he was done, "now give me what you didn't give them."

Clint studied the man for a few moments, then gave in.

"Where is this gambling establishment?" Eaton asked when he was finished.

"I don't know exactly."

Eaton gave him a look.

"I don't. I was taken there in the dark."

"How did you find your way back to the hotel from the Lutz residence?"

"I caught a cab that was out late."

"How did you and Mr. Lutz get along?"

"We didn't."

"Did he thank you for saving his wife?"

"Barely."

"Now I'm gonna ask you a hard question," Eaton said.

"Go ahead."

"What else did you and Pam Lutz do?"

"Nothing."

"Nothing?"

"Nothing."

"I find that hard to believe. I know how you are with women, my friend—more to the point, I know how women are around you. She didn't make one sexual advance toward you?"

"Well . . ."

"I knew it."

"A thank-you kiss," Clint said. "That's all it was."

"You said her dress was torn?"

"Yes."

"And you gave her your coat?"

"Yes."

"So if the coat had slipped off during the kiss . . ."

Clint found himself wondering if Eaton had been peeking through the window of the Lutz house last night.

"It slipped, but nothing happened."

"Did she ask you what hotel you were in?"

"She did."

"And you told her?"

"I did."

"Then this isn't over, my friend," Eaton said. "Not by a long shot. The lady will be back."

"Can we talk about something else now?"

"Sure," Eaton said, smiling, "tell me about James Hannigan."

TWENTY-ONE

"I can't tell you anything about that."

"Why not?"

"I don't know anything."

"You were there, right?"

"Yes."

"And you found him dead?"

"Right again."

"His throat was cut."

"You must have got this all from the police," Clint said.

"Not exactly," Eaton said, and Clint knew that the man would gladly go to jail before he revealed his source.

"Are you a suspect?" Eaton asked.

"I thought so yesterday, but now I'm not so sure."

"Why's that?"

"Lieutenant O'Grady was here this morning."

"I know O'Grady. He's a good policeman."

"I can believe that."

"What did he want to talk to you about today?"

"The same thing you want to talk about. James Hannigan."

"Didn't you tell him everything you know yesterday?" Eaton asked.

"I thought I did."

"You mean there was something else."

"Just something unimportant."

"Like what?"

Clint knew that his friend was a newspaperman first, and that everything he was telling him was for the record, but the police had not warned him not to talk to the press. So where was the harm?

He told Eaton about bumping into a man outside the building where Hannigan was killed. Eaton asked all the same questions O'Grady had asked, and Clint gave all the same answers.

"You're not being very helpful."

"Well, excuse me, but I had just seen a man with his head nearly cut off. That would shake anybody up."

"Even the Gunsmith?"

"Anyone," Clint said, fixing his friend with a hard stare, "and if you call me that in print—"

"Okay, okay," Eaton said, holding up his hands, "cease-fire. We can talk later about whether or not I can write about you."

"No, we can talk about it now."

"All right," Eaton said. "Look, the series of articles I did about the West did very well for us."

"I'm glad to hear it."

"There's only one way I can think of to top them."

"How?"

"I want to write a series about you."

"No."

"Last time I just wanted to use you in one part, now I want to do the whole series—"

"No."

Clint thought that Eaton would argue more, but the man surprised him by sitting back in his chair.

"Okay."

"What?"

"I said, okay."

"That's it? No argument?"

Eaton shook his head.

"None."

"Why?" Clint asked, looking at the man suspiciously.

"Because now I've got something else I can work on."

"You mean Hannigan?"

Eaton nodded.

"You're here in Chicago and you're involved in it. Other newspapers are gonna write about it. I have to, Clint . . . with no hard feelings, I hope."

"No," Clint said, "you're just doing your job."

"Is there anything else you can tell me?"

"No."

"Okay," Eaton said, "let's move on to a different subject."

"Like what?"

"What's this I hear that you've been offered a job with Bill Cody's Wild West Show?"

Clint stared at the man.

"What sources you have. I'm impressed."

Eaton looked sheepish.

"I'm good at my job, Clint."

"Obviously."

"Has there been an offer made?"

"I think you better ask Colonel Cody about that."

"Why not you?"

"I'm not going to say anything about it, Mark. Ask Cody."

"All right, I will." Eaton sat back. "Are we having lunch?"

"Yes, we are," Clint said, "on you."

"Well," Eaton said, "on the *Trib*."

Clint called a waiter over and they both ordered steak and potatoes.

"So tell me," Eaton said, once lunch was ordered, "are you going to see Pamela Lutz again?"

"Let me ask you a question, for a change."

"Okay, go ahead."

"What can you tell me about Philip Lutz?"

TWENTY-TWO

Clint left the hotel at six-thirty and started walking over to the Huron Gun and Hunt Club for Cody's seven o'clock show. When he got there he saw a small crowd gathered out front, and people were filing into the club. One of the men he saw out front was Mark Eaton, who had said he'd be covering the show for his newspaper.

Clint thought back to earlier that afternoon, when Eaton told him over lunch that Philip Lutz was possibly one of the most powerful men in Chicago.

"Really? I would have expected a man that powerful to live in a bigger home."

"Lutz does not spend his money unwisely. The home he has is fine with him. He's lived in it for over thirty years. In fact, his first wife decorated it."

"I see. And how long has his second wife lived in it?" Clint asked.

"Oh, Pamela's not his second wife, Clint," Eaton said, "she's his fifth."

"And all the wives have lived in that house?"

"Every one of them."

"What happened to the first wife?"

"That would be Polly. She died in that house."

"And the second, third, and fourth?"

"Divorce. Actually, in the case of the fourth wife, Patricia, she just disappeared one day. Everyone assumed she ran off with another man."

"Was there another man in the picture at the time?"

"Yes, a younger man."

"And what happened to him?"

"Nobody has seen him since."

"Wait a minute," Clint said. "The first wife's name was Polly, number four was Patricia and five is Pamela?"

"You caught on," Eaton said. "Number two was Paula and number three was Priscilla."

"Is there some reason he likes to marry women whose names start with *P*?"

"If there is—other than the fact that his own name does—he's been keeping it to himself."

"How did he manage to divorce number four . . . Patricia?"

"It took some money, but he finally managed to do it in her absence."

Lutz's business was shipbuilding, which meant he had a lot of government contracts *and* contacts. This made him even more powerful.

"Any chance of him running for office?"

"He claims not to be interested."

"Do you believe him?"

"I do," Eaton said. "If he wanted a political career

he should have started before now, when he was younger."

They finished their lunch, Eaton still pressing Clint about Pamela.

"Why are you so interested in Pamela?"

"Well, you've seen her," Eaton said. "She's beautiful. If you see her again, I want to know all about it."

"For your newspaper?"

"Hell, no," Eaton said, "for my own perverse enjoyment."

"Well," Clint had said, "I'm sure you've heard that a gentleman never kisses and tells. I may not be a gentleman, but I don't either."

Eaton saw Clint approaching now and moved to intercept him.

"Just thought I'd warn you," he said.

"About what?"

"Just before you got here, Philip and Pamela Lutz arrived."

"Oh."

"Did you tell her you were going to be here?"

"I never said a word about this," Clint said. "I didn't have time."

"Well, they're here, so be careful."

"Of what? They're both in my debt, aren't they?"

"That's just it," Eaton said. "Philip Lutz hates being in anyone's debt."

"What are all these people doing out here?" Clint asked.

"They just want to be seen before they go in."

"That's ridiculous. I'm going inside."

"I'll be out here a while longer. Doing my job, you know."

Clint nodded, worked his way through the crowd, and entered. In the lobby there was a huge poster of Buffalo Bill Cody sitting astride a horse that was standing up on its hind legs. It was a stirring picture.

"Mr. Adams."

Clint turned to see who was calling his name. It was Howard Billings.

"Hello, Mr. Billings."

"Colonel Cody asked me to keep an eye out for you, sir."

"Oh? Why?"

"He'd like to see you backstage before he goes on."

"What about?"

"He didn't tell me that."

Clint thought a moment, wondering what the man could want.

"All right, then," he said, deciding there was only one way to find out, "lead the way."

TWENTY-THREE

Clint followed Billings backstage. He was surprised to find that there was a stage to go back of in the first place. He'd gotten the impression that the Huron was just a men's club. Granted, it was a small stage, but it was a stage, nevertheless.

There was a small room in the back that Cody was apparently using as a dressing room of sorts. Billings led Clint to it and knocked on the door.

"Come in!" Cody called.

Billings opened the door and allowed Clint to go in ahead of him. He had one foot in the room himself when Cody said, "That's all, Billings. Thank you."

Billings stopped short, looked embarrassed, and then withdrew.

Cody was standing in front of a mirror, working on his beard and mustache. His outfit was all fringe and shiny bits of metal, and he looked like the grand showman Clint had always heard he was.

"Thanks for coming back here, Clint."

"No problem. Uh, why did you want me to come back here, Bill?"

Cody turned to face him.

"How do I look?" he asked.

"Women will swoon."

Cody laughed.

"I heard that Derek Mills made you an offer to perform in his theater."

"That's right."

"And you turned him down."

"Right again."

"That wasn't because of me, was it?"

"Why would you ask that?"

"I just thought since we were new friends you might be worried about competing with me."

"First of all, Bill, I don't think I could compete with you if I wanted to," Clint said. "And second of all, I don't want to."

"Well, all right, then. That's settled."

Clint didn't know what there was to settle, but he was glad Cody was satisfied.

"Now what about my offer?"

"I'm going to turn that one down, too, Bill."

"I wish you would reconsider."

"I'm sorry," Clint said. "It's just not something I could do comfortably."

"Well," Cody said, "I'm not gonna pressure you, Clint—but I want you to know the offer is open. Anytime you change your mind, you get in touch with me."

"I'll keep that in mind, Bill," Clint said. "Thanks."

"What kind of crowd did I draw tonight?" Cody asked.

"A good one. The way I hear it, you got some

pretty rich and important people out there."

"Good. I can use the extra cash. Running a show like mine ain't a cheap proposition, you know—and I hate askin' folks for money, That's why I get up on stage like this and make a fool of myself."

"I doubt you do that."

"Well, you're about to find that out firsthand, ain't you?"

"I guess I am."

"I suppose I better get out there," Cody said. "Get yourself a seat up front, Clint."

Clint looked at the man curiously.

"Bill," he asked, "you wouldn't be planning any surprises, would you?"

With an innocent look on his face, Buffalo Bill Cody replied, "Now what kind of surprise could I possibly have in mind?"

Clint stared at Cody a little longer until the man said, "Go on, get out there. I got to go on soon."

TWENTY-FOUR

Clint went out in front of the small stage and found a seat in the first row—against his better judgment. Once seated he turned to look at the crowd behind him. He spotted someone waving to him and saw that it was Pamela Lutz. Sitting to her right was her husband, and he was not waving. Clint returned the wave halfheartedly, and then continued to look around. He spotted two other faces that he recognized. One was Derek Mills, the theater owner, who inclined his head slightly. The other—surprisingly—was Lieutenant Sean O'Grady. Clint nodded, and the policeman returned the nod.

Clint started to turn when he thought he saw someone else he recognized. It was a man, and he lost him almost immediately. He tried to find him, but was interrupted when a man appeared at his left.

"May I sit here?"

He looked up and saw that it was Cody's young friend, Jerald Wilkins.

"Of course."

"Thanks."

Wilkins sat down and seemed nervous.

"Have you seen Cody do this before?" Clint asked.

"No, I haven't."

"Neither have I," Clint said. "It should be an experience."

"Yes, it should."

The young man puzzled Clint. He couldn't understand what his connection to Cody was, and he didn't know that it was his business to ask. He was almost on the verge of doing so, however, when Howard Billings appeared on the small stage.

"Ladies and gentlemen," he said, waving his hands, "we're about to begin. Please find seats, if you will."

He waited several seconds before speaking again. If anyone didn't have a seat by then, apparently it was their problem.

"Ladies and gentlemen, without further ado, our esteemed speaker, Colonel William F. Cody!"

Billings started to applaud and everyone else joined in as Cody strode out onto the stage. He started to speak.

"Ladies and gentlemen, before I start I would like to introduce someone who is in the audience tonight. He is a newly acquired friend of mine, and I'm sure most of you have heard of him. If you haven't, then you must have had your head in the sand for the past, oh, twenty years or so."

Clint was sure there were countless men in the audience who were rich and powerful and important, and who thought that Cody was talking about them. He had the uncomfortable feeling, however, that they were to be disappointed.

"Perhaps when I introduce him I can persuade him to stand. Ladies and gentlemen, a legend of the West, a friend to myself, Wild Bill Hickok, and others of the same caliber, but a man who is second to no one, I give you Clint Adams . . ."

Don't say it, Clint pleaded silently.

". . . the Gunsmith."

He said it.

Despite the fact that he was embarrassed and not a little annoyed, Clint did stand up and acknowledge the polite applause of the crowd of people, half of whom probably had no idea who he was.

He sat down, hoping that everyone would immediately forget what he looked like.

"I tried to get Mr. Adams to agree to appear on this stage with me, but he politely—and modestly—refused. I shall have to try my best to entertain you without his assistance."

Clint had to admit that for the next hour and a half he was spellbound, as was everyone else in the place. Cody had a way of talking that drew you in, and it didn't really matter what he was saying, but more how he was saying it.

When he told stories he made you feel as if you were right there with him. He told stories about buffalo hunts that made you smell the buffalo, and about Indian raids that made you fear the Indians. Clint was even more convinced that there was no way he should ever try what Cody was doing right now. He had no doubt that he would fail miserably.

At the end of the hour and a half Cody took a bow and the people stood and applauded. Clint stood and turned to look at the people behind him. He could see by their faces that they had been as entranced as he. Apparently, Cody's reputation as a showman was more than well earned.

The applause continued. Clint saw the Lutzes clapping their hands—Philip somewhat halfheartedly—and also Lieutenant O'Grady.

And then he saw that man again. He still didn't know where he'd seen him from, only that he was familiar. The other odd thing was that he was not clapping. He was simply staring up at Cody on the stage—and then Clint saw the gun and knew he had to act fast.

He leapt up onto the stage, to the surprise of Cody and the crowd.

"Clint, what the—" Cody said, but Clint hit him just as the shot rang out, both cutting the man off.

Clint and Cody fell to the ground together and the crowd was shouting and in a state of confusion. Everyone had heard the shot and those who had not wisely hit the floor were unwisely running for the exits.

In moments Clint was joined on stage by Lieutenant O'Grady.

"What happened?" the policeman demanded.

Clint looked down at Cody and saw the blood.

"He's been shot," he said, "Colonel Cody's been shot."

TWENTY-FIVE

Quickly Clint gave O'Grady as accurate a description as he could of the man who had shot Cody, and O'Grady left the stage as swiftly as he had arrived.

"Cody?" Clint said. "Bill, are you all right?"

"Damned if I'm all right, man. I've been shot, haven't I?"

"Let's get you off the stage before you get shot again."

Clint helped him up and in doing so saw that Cody's wound was in his shoulder. A few more inches, and it would have been the heart.

He helped the injured man backstage and into the small dressing room. In moments there were footsteps outside and both Billings and Wilkins appeared.

"Is he all right?" Billings asked.

"Get a doctor," Clint said.

"But I only—"

"Get a doctor!"

Billings backed off and ran for a doctor.

"Jerald, keep everyone out. Understood? No one comes in except a doctor, or a policeman."

"Right," Wilkins said firmly.

Clint closed the door and then went to where Cody was sitting.

"Damn fool thing . . ." Cody said.

Clint helped him off with his jacket, then tore the shirt so he could see the wound.

"It looks bad," Clint said.

"Not as bad as it might have been. You move pretty quick, Clint. How did you know?"

"I was watching the crowd, and I thought I saw a man I recognized."

"From where?"

"I'm not sure, but the next thing I knew he had a gun pointed at you."

"Well, I'm just glad he shot me after my performance," Cody said. "That means I still get paid."

"Just sit quiet. A doctor should be here soon."

"You saved my life, you know."

"I didn't have much of a choice."

Cody sat back in his chair. His face was pale and waxy-looking.

"Damn," he said, closing his eyes, "I guess at least one person didn't like my stories, huh?"

"Have you been having trouble with anybody lately?" Clint asked.

"Nobody I thought was in Chicago."

"Did you see anyone in the audience you knew?"

"Nobody I didn't expect to see."

Clint looked around for something to use to stem the flow of blood. When he didn't find anything, he just tore Cody's shirt to shreds and used it to fashion some kind of bandage. As Clint tightened it, Cody winced.

"Sorry."

"Don't be. It's only because of you that I'm around to feel pain. I'm grateful."

"Where the hell is that doctor?" Clint wondered aloud.

At that moment there was a knock on the door. When Clint opened it, Wilkins said, "There's a Lieutenant O'Grady here with a doctor."

"Okay," Clint said, opening the door wide, "let them in."

O'Grady came in followed by a man carrying a doctor's bag.

"This is Doctor Kramer," O'Grady said. "Somebody remembered that he only lived a few blocks away."

Kramer was in his fifties and appeared to be trying to wake up. He yawned as he crouched down in front of Cody.

"Let me have a look," he said. "Who put this bandage on?"

"I did," Clint said.

"Nice field dressing."

"Thanks. I've had some experience."

"Colonel Cody, can you answer some questions?"

"Not now. Lieutenant," Kramer said. "Let me see the extent of the damage."

"Clint Adams knows more than I do, Lieutenant," Cody said. "Clint? Would you mind?"

"I'll take care of it, Bill."

"Let's go out in the hall," O'Grady suggested.

They went outside with Jerald Wilkins and closed the door.

"Who's this? O'Grady asked.

Clint told him the young man's name.

"He's a friend of Cody's."

Apparently that satisfied O'Grady. He turned his full attention to Clint.

"Tell me what happened. What you saw."

Quickly Clint told O'Grady everything.

"And you knew him?"

"I didn't know him," Clint said, "but I had seen him somewhere before."

"Where?"

"I don't—wait a minute. Yes! I remember now," Clint said excitedly as the memory of where he had first seen the man came back.

"Let me in on it," O'Grady said.

"Outside of the building where Hannigan was killed," Clint said. "He was the man I bumped into."

"What?"

"Yes, I'm sure of it."

"Wait a minute. You're saying that the same man who killed James Hannigan tried to kill Cody?"

"No, I'm not saying that," Clint said. "I'm just saying that I saw him outside of Hannigan's building. We don't know he killed him."

"But we do know that he tried to kill Cody."

"Yes."

"I'll have some men go back to that area and do a house-to-house. There's a dirty little hotel right next to Hannigan's building. Maybe the man has a room there."

"If he does tonight," Clint said, "he won't by morning."

O'Grady rubbed his jaw.

"You're probably right. I'd better get over there with some men tonight."

"Let me know what happens."

"Uh-uh," O'Grady said, shaking his head.

"Why not?"

"Because you're the only one who can identify him," O'Grady said.

"Wha—"

"You're coming with me," O'Grady said, grabbing Clint's elbow. "Come on."

TWENTY-SIX

It was dawn when Clint returned to the hotel in the company of Sean O'Grady.

"You kept me up all night," Clint said, "You owe me breakfast for that."

"I'm too hungry to argue," O'Grady said, and they went directly to the dining room.

"We're not quite ready to open, gentlemen," the waiter told them.

O'Grady took out his badge and said, "Get ready."

The waiter smiled nervously and said, "I'll tell the cook."

"Tell him steak and eggs," O'Grady said. "That okay?"

"Fine," Clint said.

"Two," O'Grady said, and the waiter nodded. "And bring coffee right away."

The waiter nodded again and went off to fill the order.

Clint and O'Grady sat down heavily at a table and stared at each other.

"I guess he didn't wait to do it the way you said," O'Grady remarked. "Instead of shooting Cody and then checking out, he checked out first."

"Looks that way."

"That clerk's lying." O'Grady said. The clerk at the hotel claimed not to recognize the description of the man that Clint had given him.

"Probably just afraid."

"Of the police, or the killer?"

"Both."

The waiter came over with a pot of coffee and two cups. He poured, his hand shaking, and then moved away from the table. Clint and O'Grady drank gratefully.

"What will you do now?" Clint asked.

"About the killer?"

"You keep calling him that," Clint said. "You still don't know that he killed Hannigan."

"What else am I to think? That it was a coincidence that you bumped into him outside the building?"

"It could have been."

"Do you believe in coincidence, Clint?"

"No, but—"

"You didn't strike me as the kind of man who would."

"But why would he kill Hannigan and then stay around the building?"

"I don't know," O'Grady said. "I don't know why the criminal mind does anything—especially killers. They're not just criminal minds, they're insane."

Clint remained silent, but he still didn't accept the theory that the man who had shot Cody was the same man who had killed James Hannigan. It just didn't feel right to him.

"As for what I'm going to do, I'll give his description to every policeman in Chicago. We'll cover the trains, and the docks. He won't get out of town."

"What if he just walks out?"

"I don't think he will."

"Why not?"

"Because he *didn't* kill Cody," O'Grady said. "He tried and missed. I don't think he's going to accept that."

That much Clint agreed with. The man had taken a huge chance to kill Cody in a roomful of people. There was no reason to think that he wouldn't try again.

Except for one thing . . .

"Your only chance to get him is if he tries again," Clint said.

"Right."

"Cody may not be able to keep his other engagements."

"A showman like him? I think he will. After all the stories he told tonight, do you think a bullet in the shoulder is going to stop him?"

"You didn't believe all those stories, did you, Lieutenant?"

O'Grady glanced at Clint a bit sheepishly.

"Well . . . some of them."

"Some of them," Clint said, "were half true, and some were not true at all."

"But he *was* an army scout and a buffalo hunter, wasn't he?"

"Well, yes."

"How do you know his stories aren't true?"

"Well, I don't, but—"

"How many of the stories about you are true?"

"A few, but—"

"It only takes a few to impress someone who's never been out west," O'Grady said.

"Like you?"

O'Grady hesitated, then said, "I admit I enjoyed his stories."

"Well, I admit that," Clint said. "True or untrue, the man is a masterful storyteller."

"No argument there."

The waiter came with their breakfasts then, huge plates with steak, eggs, and spuds.

"Biscuits," O'Grady said.

"Coming up," the waiter said, and hurried off to get them. He returned with a basket of fresh baked biscuits. Both Clint and O'Grady gave all their attention to their food until the plates were empty and the waiter had brought a second pot of coffee.

"I almost feel alive," O'Grady said, "except for the grit in my eyes."

"Do you have a wife to explain this to?" Clint asked.

"No." O'Grady said, "no wife." He didn't elaborate, so Clint didn't know if the man was single, divorced, or widowed. He decided not to ask.

"I'm going to go up to my room and catch a few hours sleep," Clint said. "Then I'll check on Cody."

"Is he in this hotel?"

"Yes."

"Good. I can check on both of you at the same time." Clint frowned.

"Why would you want to check on me?"

"You're my only witness, Clint," O'Grady said.

"You saw the man outside Hannigan's building and then again when he shot Cody."

"You think he's going to come after me?" Clint asked. "He probably doesn't even know who I am."

"You forget," O'Grady said, "thanks to Cody everyone who was there last night knows who you are—and that includes the killer."

"Shit," Clint said. He had forgotten that.

O'Grady stood up.

"I'll put some men inside and outside the hotel to keep an eye on you and Cody. Who knows, the crazy fool might actually try to get to one or both of you here."

"I hope he does."

"Do you have a gun?"

Clint had the New Line in the back of his belt, but he said, "Up in my room."

"Well," O'Grady said, "if you quote me I'll deny I said this, but you might want to carry it."

"I'll keep that in mind."

"Ready to go?"

"I'm going to finish this pot of coffee."

O'Grady nodded and put some money down on the table.

"That should be enough to cover breakfast. I'll probably see you in a few hours."

"If I'm awake."

"Yeah," the policeman said, "I know how you feel."

"Thanks for breakfast."

"Thanks for your cooperation."

Clint laughed.

"As is I had a choice."

O'Grady laughed and left the dining room.

Clint thought back to the night before when Cody had introduced him and made him stand up. If only he'd remained seated the killer wouldn't know who he was and what he looked like.

That is, if he hadn't known already from their brief encounter in front of James Hannigan's building. Had the killer—if indeed he was the killer—registered seeing him there? Was that why he had already checked out of the hotel? And where was the crazy bastard now?

Clint had one thing going for him. Even if the killer knew him on sight, he would recognize the killer as well.

Starting out even, Clint Adams always figured he had the edge.

TWENTY-SEVEN

The killer entered his new hotel room and locked the door behind him. Luckily, the voice had told him to check out of his old hotel before going after Buffalo Bill Cody. He was sure the police had gone there immediately after the shooting. He laughed at the thought of them finding out that he had eluded them.

He did not laugh, however, when he thought about Clint Adams saving Cody's life. If Adams had not tackled Cody, the great man would have been shot right through the heart.

But he laughed again when he realized how, inadvertently, Cody had helped him identify the man who had ruined his shot. It was, in fact, the same man who had bumped into him near his first hotel. Initially he was worried about why Clint Adams had been there, but a quick check of the newspapers told him why. There had been a murder in the building next to his hotel. That's where Adams had been. It had nothing to do with him.

Saving Cody, though, that Clint Adams had to pay
for. The killer didn't know how, though. That
wouldn't be up to him. That was up to the voice.

The killer sat on the bed and checked his gun. He
knew that most assassins had fancy guns, but for him
his father's old Navy Colt worked just fine. In fact,
he'd used that very gun to kill his father. The old
man had been beating on his mother, and he just up
and grabbed the gun and put two bullets in the old
man's back. To his surprise his mother—whom he
had saved—started yelling and screaming at him, so
he killed her, too.

Once it started it just kept going . . .

That was the first night he had heard the voice.
Not after killing his father, but after his mother. The
voice told him that he had to kill his brother and
sister, too.

His brother made it easy. He came running in from
the fields when he heard the shots, and before he
could say anything the killer shot him, too.

That left his younger sister.

She was only twelve and at first he resisted the
voice, but he soon learned that resistance was futile.
The voice just kept getting louder and louder in his
head until he couldn't stand it anymore.

His sister, having heard the shots, was hiding under her bed, but that didn't stop the killer. He fired
two shots right through her thin mattress. When he
pulled her from beneath the bed, she was bleeding
but still alive. She looked up at him and opened her
mouth—probably to ask, "Why?"—but he never
gave her a chance. He fired two more times, and it
was done.

Now he ejected the spent shell from the Colt and replaced it with a live round. That done he sat cross-legged on the bed, with the gun in his lap, and awaited the appearance of the voice to tell him what to do next.

TWENTY-EIGHT

Clint went up to his room with intentions of going right to sleep. What he found there surprised him and, yes, even woke him up.

Hell, seeing Pamela Lutz naked would wake up a dead man!

And there she was, naked in his bed, asleep as he entered, but his appearance woke her and she sat straight up. Apparently she was one of those people who woke up immediately alert.

"Where have you been?"

She might have been a wife asking her husband why he had been out so late.

"I had some things to take care of," he said, staring at her. "I was with the police."

"They didn't arrest you, did they?" she asked, concerned. "I know Philip talked to the mayor—"

"No, they didn't arrest me. I was trying to help them find the man who shot Cody last night."

"Wasn't that awful?" she asked. "But you were

112

wonderful! You saved Buffalo Bill's life. Was he very grateful?"

"Extremely grateful."

"That's good. He should be—"

"Pamela," he said finally, "what are you doing here?"

"I'm here for you, silly."

"Does your husband know where you are?"

"No," she said. "He probably thinks I'm gambling."

"From where I'm standing," Clint said, "it would seem that you are. Aren't you afraid that he'll divorce you?"

"Oh, he will," she said. "He always divorces his wives, but not until he's good and ready."

"And he's not ready yet?"

She shook her head.

"He's not even close to being ready."

She shook her head again.

"That is one thing Philip has never done."

"Well, there's always a first time."

That's when she dropped the sheet away from her, revealing her naked breasts. They were as full and round as he remembered, and even more lovely.

"For everything," she said.

"Pamela," Clint said, unable to keep his eyes off her breasts, "you're a beautiful woman—"

"That line is usually followed by a 'but,' " she said. "The only butt I want to hear is yours hitting these sheets."

That surprised Clint. She saw that and liked it.

"Not the way you're used to hearing a woman talk, is it?" she asked.

"No."

"Are you afraid of my husband?"

"No."

"I'm sure you've heard things about him."

"Just that he has money." Clint said, "and he's been checking up on me."

"Oh, he knows all about you." She wrapped her arms around her knees, hiding her breasts from sight.

"Really?"

She nodded.

"And he told me everything."

"Why?"

"He was trying to convince me that you were very dangerous."

"And did he succeed?"

"I didn't need convincing," Pam said. "I knew you were dangerous the first time I saw you at the club."

"You saw me at the club? I thought you were concentrating on your game."

She smiled slowly and said, "I was."

"There's something I want to ask you."

"Why don't you get comfortable first?"

"Let me ask the question first."

"All right."

"Those two men the other night? Did you know them?"

"No." Her answer was immediate, no hesitation. Her eyes were steady, as was her voice. "You think I set that whole thing up?"

"The thought had crossed my mind."

She rubbed her hands over her upper arms. The motion was very sensual to Clint. The smell of her was reaching him, too, and he felt his body beginning to react.

"I'll tell you a secret," she said.

"I'm listening."

"I noticed you the minute you walked in that night. From that point on I couldn't concentrate on my game."

"You won," he said. "I saw you cash out."

"I was further ahead before you arrived. I recouped some of it before I left, but from the moment you walked in I lost money."

"Well . . . that's flattering."

"I kept waiting for you to come over to me."

"I didn't want to interrupt your gambling," he said. "I, uh, didn't know that I already had."

"Well, when you didn't come over I decided nothing was going to happen, so I left. Those two men followed me and pulled me into that alley. That's when you came along."

"Luckily."

"I don't think luck had anything to do with it," she said. "I think fate was responsible."

"Fate?"

"Don't you believe in fate?"

"I've never thought much about it."

"That was your first night in Chicago, right?"

"Yes."

"What do you think the chances were that we'd meet that night, your first night here, in a place you didn't even know existed until you first walked in?"

"I don't know."

"It was fate," she said. She unwound her arms from her knees and leaned back, resting her weight on her arms. The position pushed her breasts out toward him. He noticed that her nipples were erect and hard.

"What were the chances I'd end up in your bed this morning?"

"Even higher."

"Oh, no," she said. "The odds were very good."

"This wouldn't make your husband very happy."

"No, it wouldn't, but I learned something very soon after I married my husband."

"What was that?"

"I learned that he is not a very happy man, and that there's little I can do to change that. So I decided that I should do what I could to keep myself happy. Is that so wrong? Wanting to be happy?"

"Well . . . no . . ."

"Don't you want to be happy?"

"Of course."

She slid one hand softly down between her breasts.

"Why don't you come over here, Clint, and we can make each other very happy?"

He watched as her hand came around beneath one of her big breasts and cupped it.

Hell, he thought, why not?

TWENTY-NINE

The killer watched as the girl undressed. The desk clerk had sent her up, just a half hour after he asked for a whore.

"I got some nice girls—" the man had started to say, but the killer had cut him off.

"I want a whore."

"Well, okay," the clerk said, "I got some nice whores, too. I'll send one up."

The killer went to his room and waited.

The voice told him to get a girl and enjoy himself. It wasn't often the voice told him to have sex. In fact, a lot of times he'd want a girl—a specific girl—and the voice would tell him no. That's because the voice knew that he sometimes got carried away and hurt the girl—sometimes even killed her.

The girl had her dress down around her ankles and was now removing her black underwear. She was young, in her early twenties, and her breasts were large, almost pendulous. They swayed as she bent over to remove her underpants and his eyes went to the black bush between her legs.

He wasn't going to kill the girl this time, though. The voice had told him not to. He was just supposed to have sex with her and enjoy himself. This, the voice said, would cleanse him and prepare him for his next move.

The killer was surprised that the voice was not angry with him for having failed to kill Buffalo Bill Cody. This time, it was very understanding. After all, who expected this man Clint Adams to interfere?

The girl was naked now.

"Aren't you going to undress?" she asked.

"Lie on the bed," he commanded.

She was pretty. He liked that. A lot of whores were ugly. Maybe this one would be ugly when she got older. Maybe her breasts would sag and hang to her knees. Yes, that's probably what would happen. Maybe he'd be doing the girl a favor by killing her.

"Like this?" she asked, lying on her side.

She wasn't so pretty that way. Her breasts hung in a funny way.

"On your back," he said, "lie on your back."

She rolled onto her back and her big breasts flattened against her chest. That was better.

"Are you gonna get undressed, honey?" she asked.

"Yes," he said, staring at her, convinced that he would be doing her a kindness if he killed her, "yes, I am going to undress."

THIRTY

As tired as Clint was, he was impressed with his performance. Of course, much of it had to do with his partner. Pamela Lutz was an exciting woman. She was innovative and free, open to anything. Together they explored all of the possibilities that existed between a man and a woman, and then they invented some.

The last time they made love it was after noon, and it was a slow and gentle good-bye. She had to get back home. She said she didn't really want to test her husband's limits just yet.

She told him this while she was astride him. He was buried deep inside of her, and when she clenched her muscles it was like she was grabbing him tightly. Earlier, he had entered her from behind, her perfect buttocks pushed tightly into his belly. She was on her hands and knees but looking back at him over her shoulder with a look on her face he found exciting, but hard to describe. At that time she had also been clenching and unclenching, and he supposed that the look said, "You think you have me, but I have you."

Frankly, Clint didn't care who had who, he was just happy they were having each other.

He surprised her that final time, rolling over with her until they were lying side by side, and he made love to her that way until she closed her eyes, arched her back, and surrendered to the sensations that flooded her body.

Right at that moment—just before his own orgasm—he put his mouth to her ear and said, "I have you. . . ."

Later, as she dressed, she said, "You're a bastard, you know."

"Am I?"

"Oh, yes," she said. "A lovely, wonderful, sweet bastard."

"I guess if I have to be one," he said, "that's the kind to be."

When she was fully dressed she came and sat on the bed next to him. She ran her hand over his belly, and then down beneath the sheet to hold him lightly.

"I don't know if I'll be able to come back."

"I know."

"I don't even know if I can get out to go to the club," she said. "I might have to pay dearly for this morning."

"You mean—"

"No, no," she said, laughing, "Philip has never struck me. He wouldn't dare. How sweet you are." She leaned over and kissed him. "No, I just mean I might have to behave myself for a while."

"I understand."

She released him and slapped him on the stomach hard. It stung.

"Hey!"

"Why are you so damned understanding? Argue with me. Tell me you want to see me."

"You're married, Pamela," he said. "Even if I want to see you again, we would have to do it at your convenience, wouldn't we?"

"Have you ever been married?"

"No."

"Haven't you ever been with a married woman before?"

He hesitated, then said, "Yes."

"Then why are you so disapproving of it?"

"To tell you the truth, I don't know."

"Is marriage sacred to you? Is that it?"

"How can it be sacred to me if I've never been married?"

"Marriage is not perfect, Clint," she said. "Lots of people get married and find out they don't love each other. Most of them stay married, and faithful—and unhappy. I don't intend to be unhappy. Can you blame me for that?"

"I guess not."

She kissed him shortly and walked to the door.

"We'll see each other again."

"Hey, wait a minute!"

She stopped with the door half open.

"How did you know I'd be at the Huron Club last night?" he asked.

"I didn't," she said. "Philip had been planning to attend ever since he heard that Buffalo Bill Cody was going to be there."

"Is he planning on attending any of Cody's other performances?"

"I don't know," she said. "Will there be other performances, after what happened last night?"

"I don't know. I have to check on Cody later today."

"Well, if there are," she said, smiling playfully, "maybe we'll see you there."

When she left, Clint rolled over and buried his face in the pillow. It smelled of her. This was one of his favorite times, savoring the scent of a woman he'd slept with after she'd gone. It was as if she was still with him in a way.

He rolled onto his back and stared at the ceiling. Sleeping with married women had never bothered him. It usually meant they were unhappy, and being with him made them happy. What was wrong with that?

Or was he just getting too old for that kind of self-serving logic? Would he even have thought of it as self-serving ten years ago? Five? Last year?

He closed his eyes and when he opened them again it was four p.m.

THIRTY-ONE

Clint left his room with intentions of checking in with Cody to see how he was. He was in the hall outside his own room when he realized he didn't know Cody's room number.

He went down to the front desk and asked for Cody's room number.

"I—I'm not supposed to give that out, sir," the clerk said nervously.

"Who said?"

He saw the clerk's eyes flick behind him and turned to find a man watching him from about ten feet away. The man was tall, young—in his late twenties—and was wearing a three-piece suit.

"Police?" Clint asked.

The clerk nodded.

Clint walked over to the policeman.

"Do you know who I am?"

"Yes, sir," the policeman said. "You're Mr. Adams."

"That's right. Why are you here?"

"For your protection, sir, and the protection of Colonel Cody."

"I'd like to see how Colonel Cody is doing, but the clerk won't give me his room number. Do you have any objection to my having it?"

The man thought a moment, then said, "Well, no, sir."

"Would you get it for me, then?"

"Sure."

They walked to the desk together, and the policeman asked the clerk for Cody's room number. The man hesitated, looking at Clint.

"It's all right," the policeman said.

The clerk gave him the room number.

"Thank you," Clint said to the policeman.

"You're welcome."

"There was no policeman outside my door."

"We have no orders to be outside your door, sir."

"Is there someone outside of Colonel Cody's?"

"Yes, sir."

"Will he know who I am?"

"I'm sure he will, sir."

"Good," Clint said, "I don't want to get shot while paying a condolence call."

The man didn't smile.

"You won't, sir."

"Can you describe the policeman upstairs for me, please?"

The man did. Clint nodded and went back up the stairs. Cody was on the floor above his. As he entered the hall, he saw a man sitting in a chair outside one of the doors. He assumed this was the policeman assigned to watch Cody's room.

Clint approached the man, who spotted him and stood up. He was the same age and dressed the same way as the man downstairs.

"Hello, Mr. Adams."

"Could you do me a favor, officer?"

"Sure, if I can." The man frowned.

"Could you describe the policeman in the lobby?"

The man did, and the description fit perfectly.

"How is Colonel Cody doing?"

"I don't know, sir."

"Has the doctor been here?"

"Yes."

"Did you ask about the colonel's condition?"

"No, sir."

"Why not?"

The policeman frowned again.

"That's not my job, sir."

"All right. Is the door unlocked?"

"Yes, sir. I don't suppose the colonel would be able to get up and let you in."

"I don't suppose he would."

Clint knocked and opened the door even before Cody called out, "Come in."

Clint looked toward the bed and was surprised to find it empty. He looked around the room and found Cody sitting in a chair by the window, dressed—after a fashion. He was wearing trousers and a shirt, but no boots.

"Clint. By God, man, where have you been? I need something decent to eat."

Clint closed the door.

"I needed to get some sleep. I was up all night trying to help the police find the man who shot you."

"Did you find the bounder?"

"No. We found the hotel he was in, but he checked out."

"But you know his name?"

"No. It's not the kind of hotel where you sign your name in a register."

"Damn! I'd like to know who this fella is and what he has against me."

"Shouldn't you be in bed?"

"I've been in that bed all night and most of the day. Any longer and I'll sprout roots."

"How are you feeling?"

"Fit," Cody said. "The doctor got the bullet out and patched me up. There's no permanent damage."

"Well, that's good."

"Thanks to you, I'll say again."

"And for the last time, I hope."

"All right," Cody said, "but never let it be said I'm not a grateful man."

"Done."

"Now get me something decent to eat, man!" It was a plea.

Clint opened the door and said to the policeman, "Would you get Colonel Cody some steak and eggs, please?"

"I, uh, can't leave here, sir—"

"I'll stay here with him until you get back."

"I . . . don't know . . ."

"I'll take full responsibility. I'll explain it to Lieutenant O'Grady."

"Well . . . all right."

"Thanks. Also some coffee and a few cups so you can have some."

"Thank you, sir."

Clint nodded and closed the door.

"Food's on the way."

"Good."

"I guess you'll be canceling your other perform-ances, huh?"

"Hell no."

Clint laughed, not sure Cody was being serious.

"You're kidding. How can you—"

"I can stand," Cody said. "That's all I have to be able to do, stand and talk. Why should I miss out on the revenue I'd be bringing in? I need that money."

"But you can't . . . what if the killer tries again?"

"There'll be police."

"What if you keel over?"

"It will be part of the show."

"You're crazy."

"Maybe, but I'm not letting some little coward who shot me from hiding keep me from doing what I do . . . unless . . ."

"Unless what?" Clint asked suspiciously.

"Unless we can figure out a way for me to stay here, but still get paid."

"And how would you do that?"

"I wouldn't," Cody said, looking at Clint, "you would."

THIRTY-TWO

"Oh no—"

"Hear me out."

"I don't have to hear you out," Clint said. "I know what you've got in mind."

"All you'd have to do is take my place for a couple of nights, until I get my strength back."

"A couple of nights? How many nights do you have speaking engagements planned for?"

"Seven. Tonight's has been postponed until to-morrow at three, and then I'm to do Derek Mills's theater at seven. You could do both of those for me."

"No."

"I'll split the money with you."

"No."

"Fifty-fifty."

"No."

"All right, sixty-forty."

"No!"

"Is this how you treat a friend?"

"We're not friends. We've only just met."

"I make friends quickly."

"Well, I don't"

"You're a liar."

Clint stared at Cody and said, "Yes, I am, but just because we're friends does not mean I'm going to go onstage and make a fool of myself."

"You won't make a fool of yourself," Cody said. "Tell a story. Tell about something you did with Wyatt Earp or Bat Masterson. They are friends of yours, aren't they?"

"Yes, but—"

"And you've had adventures together?"

Clint laughed.

"Many."

"Well, then, you've got countless resources for stories. Just tell a few and the people will eat it up, especially Easterners. They'll believe anything."

"Wait a minute," Clint said, "I can't lie—"

"No, no, man, I'm not saying lie, I'm saying . . . *embellish*."

"That's lying."

"No, it's dressing the truth up so it will look and sound prettier and more interesting."

"Lying."

"All right, then," Cody said, "lie a little. It won't hurt."

"Cody—"

"Clint," Cody said, "if you don't do this for me I'll do it myself."

"You're blackmailing me."

"Yes."

There was a knock on the door then and Clint

opened it to find Lieutenant Sean O'Grady standing in the hall.

"You weren't in your room, and my man in the lobby said you didn't leave. Then he told me you came up here. Where's the man supposed to be here?"

"I sent him for some food. Cody was hungry."

"How is he?" O'Grady asked.

"Come in and see for yourself."

Clint backed away from the door and O'Grady entered.

"You fellas haven't been introduced," Clint said. "William F. Cody meet Lieutenant Sean O'Grady. The lieutenant was the second man up onstage last night."

"Clint tells me you two were up all night looking for the man who shot me. I'm grateful, sir."

"I guess he also told you we failed?"

"No matter," Cody said, waving with his good hand. "You did your best, and I appreciate it."

"Why were you looking for me?" Clint asked.

"Just wanted to ask you some more questions."

"Well, let's wait for your man to get back and then we can go talk."

"Talk here," Cody said. "Unless there's something secret going on?"

"No," O'Grady said, passing a hand over his face, "nothing secret."

"You look terrible," Clint said. "Did you get any sleep?"

"About an hour, and then they woke me up because they found a dead prostitute."

"Too bad."

"Worse than that. She was mauled, slashed, bitten . . . what a mess."

"Just what you need," Clint said sympathetically.

"I'm sorry you have to be caught up in my business when you've got something like that to be looking after," Cody said.

"It's all part of the job, Colonel."

There was another knock then and it was the policeman with the food. When he saw his superior there he blanched.

"Bring the food in, Foster," O'Grady said. "We'll talk later."

"Uh, yes, sir."

Foster laid the tray on the night table and hurried for the door.

"Foster, I promised you some coffee," Clint said.

"That's all right, sir. Thanks, anyway."

Clint looked at O'Grady and said, "Well, now that you scared the poor man away you might as well have his coffee."

"Thanks," O'Grady said, "I think I will."

THIRTY-THREE

Over coffee Clint, Cody, and O'Grady talked about the previous day's incidents. It was the first chance the policeman had to talk to Cody about it. While they talked, Cody ate, insisting that he could cut his own meat and feed himself. He did so laboriously.

"And you didn't see anything?" O'Grady asked.

"I saw a lot of people standing and applauding," Cody said. "Unfortunately, when that is going on I don't make it a point to look at each and every person."

"What about when the shot was fired?"

"By that time I saw Clint coming toward me. I wasn't looking out into the crowd at all. I'm afraid Clint knows more than I do about the whole thing."

"Well, then, can you tell me who would want to kill you?"

Cody stared at O'Grady helplessly.

"Lots of people, or maybe no one. I don't know. I've probably made a lot of enemies over the years, but I wouldn't expect to find any of them here."

"What about recently?" O'Grady asked. "Maybe somebody you fired from your show?"

"I haven't fired anyone in over a year. Things have been going remarkably well for a little more than that. I'm sorry, Lieutenant, I wish I could help you. I want you to find the man who shot me, I truly do."

"I know, Colonel Cody, and we'll do our best to do so," O'Grady said. He turned to Clint and asked, "What are your plans for today?"

Before Clint could answer, Cody said, "He's going to work on his performance."

"What performance?" O'Grady asked.

"Don't listen to him."

"He's taking my place at two of my performances tomorrow," Cody said.

"You are?" O'Grady asked in surprise.

"Don't listen to him."

"He is."

"Did I walk into something here?" O'Grady asked.

"Yes, you did," Clint said.

"No, you didn't" Cody said.

"Well, I—" O'Grady started.

"He wants me to keep my engagements even though I'm gravely wounded," Cody said.

"I never said that!"

"Well, he won't replace me, and I can't cancel, so I'll have to go on myself—at high risk to my safety and health."

"You said there would be police there to protect you," Clint said.

"Ah, but my wound could flare up. There could be infection. I could die onstage. What would you say then?" Cody demanded.

Clint glared at him and said, "I'd say they got more than they paid for."

After a beat Clint looked at O'Grady and asked, "What are your plans?"

"I've got to work on this prostitute that was found dead. She's the third one this month. I'm afraid we have a madman on our hands."

"Two," Cody said.

"What are the chances you'd have two madmen in the city during the same month?" Clint asked O'Grady.

"I would have said slim, had you asked me that last month."

"Are you two going to talk in here all day?" Cody had stopped eating with the meal half gone.

"You told us to talk here."

"Well, now I'm asking you to take it someplace else," Cody said, rising from the chair. "I'm suddenly very fatigued."

"It's no wonder, with that wound," O'Grady said.

"Don't give him any sympathy," Clint said. "He'll use it against me."

Cody slipped into bed and said to Clint, "You should be off trying to decide what you're going to say tomorrow afternoon, and then tomorrow night."

"I'm not going to say anything!"

"I'll have Billings contact you and let you know the arrangements."

"Cody—"

"I'm sleepy." He lay down and pulled the sheet up to his chin.

"We'd better go," O'Grady said. "He needs his rest."

"I have my doubts," Clint said, but he followed O'Grady out of the room.

THIRTY-FOUR

Clint and O'Grady headed down to the lobby. Before leaving, though, O'Grady lagged behind and talked to the policeman named Foster.

On the way down the stairs Clint said, "I told Foster that if he went for the food I'd take full responsibility."

"That's noble," O'Grady said, "but my instructions were for him not to leave his post under any circumstances, and my instructions supercede yours or anyone else's."

"What are you going to do to him?"

"Nothing," O'Grady said, "I just gave him a talking-to. If he does it again, though—"

"Why do I get the feeling you're not as tough as you like to make out?" Clint asked.

"I don't know," O'Grady said, scowling, "why is it?"

Clint decided not to pursue the line.

"Where is Sergeant Folkes, by the way?"

"He's working on the dead prostitute," O'Grady said.

"Let's talk about this madman theory again," Clint said.

"What about it?"

"Two in Chicago in the same month?"

"What are you saying? That there's only one madman? He kills women, cuts them up, chews up pieces of them, and spits them out at the scene—"

"God!" Clint said, touching his stomach. "And they say the West is uncivilized?"

"Then this same maniac decides to try to kill Buffalo Bill Cody?" O'Grady continued. "Why would he do that?"

"Why would anyone do either one of those things?" Clint asked.

O'Grady shook his head as they reached the lobby.

"It's too much of a coincidence, Clint," he said. "I can't see it."

"How are you going to work both cases then?"

"I'll oversee both," O'Grady said.

"Tell me, which one do your superiors want you to work?"

O'Grady stopped walking and turned to face Clint.

"They think that Cody is the more important of the two. On one hand you have a living legend of the West, and on the other a dead whore. Which would you think is more important?"

"In your place? I'd consider the whore."

O'Grady frowned.

"Why?"

"Because Cody will be gone soon. He'll move on. What happens if this madman stops killing whores and decides to kill decent women?"

"It doesn't make a difference to me whether the women are considered decent or not," O'Grady said. "He's killed three, and I don't want to see any more."

"But Cody's an important man, and your superiors are worried that if something happens to him it will look bad for them?"

"Exactly."

Clint shook his head and said, "Politics."

"Exactly!" O'Grady said with more feeling.

"It never changes, does it?" Clint asked. "No matter if you're a lawman in a small western town or a large eastern city. It's the politicians who run everything."

"That's right," O'Grady said. "You were a lawman for a while, weren't you?"

"A long time ago."

"Have you ever run into anything like this?"

"The killer, you mean?"

O'Grady nodded.

"I was in London, England, some time ago when a man was strangling women."

"Did they catch him?"

"Yes."

O'Grady shook his head.

"I hope we catch this one."

"Do you have anything that might lead you to him?"

O'Grady looked around the lobby, then over toward the bar.

"Come on," he said, "I'll buy you a drink and tell you about it. Maybe you can come up with something I haven't thought of."

THIRTY-FIVE

So far, O'Grady explained, the killer had murdered and mutilated three women during a four-week period. They were all prostitutes, and all were found in different areas.

"Not different parts of the city, though," O'Grady said. "See, I think he's right around here somewhere. Michigan Avenue, Rush Street, Huron Street . . . the downtown area."

"Why wouldn't he move around? By staying in one area he's increasing the chances that he'll be caught."

"Only we haven't even come close to catching him," O'Grady said. "I've increased foot patrols, but nothing seems to help."

"Have you checked all the hotels in the area?"

"Yes, but we can't look in every room."

"These whores who have been killed," Clint asked, "are they expensive girls?"

"No," O'Grady said, "they're the kind of girls you'd find all up and down Rush Street."

"Why don't you put a woman on the street and see what happens?"

"What do you mean?"

"Do you have any women in your police department?"

"Well, yes, but they don't work on the street."

"Put one on the street then. Dress her as a cheap whore."

"And what happens when she gets killed?"

"Well, have a couple of men watching her. If she gets picked up by a man, they can follow her. If it turns out to be the wrong man, then she tries again."

"Are you saying she should actually . . . prostitute herself?"

"No," Clint said. "Your men can check out any man who picks her up. She can make them think she's going to service them, just long enough to see what their intentions are."

O'Grady sat back in his chair and toyed with his beer mug.

"You know, I like it," he said finally.

"All you need is a woman who is young enough, attractive enough—in a cheap sort of way—and willing to take the chance."

O'Grady looked at Clint and then smiled slowly.

"I think I know just the woman." He stood up quickly and said, "I've got to go. By God, this is a good idea!"

"It's yours," Clint said, "free of charge."

"Oh, are you going to take Cody's place tomorrow or what?"

"What do you think?"

"I think you should do it."

Clint made a face.

"Talk to the doctor before you make up your mind, why don't you?" O'Grady suggested.

"Now that's a good idea. What was his name?"

"Kramer, Doctor Kramer."

"Do you have an address on him?"

"No, I only know that he lived near the Huron Club. Somebody over there might be able to tell you where he lives."

"That's a good idea, Lieutenant.

"Sean," O'Grady said, "and one good turn deserves another, doesn't it?"

"Will you let me know what happens with my idea?"

"If we catch this bastard," O'Grady said, "you'll be the first to know."

"Good luck."

"Thanks."

Clint watched O'Grady walk out of the bar and then stayed to finish his own beer. While he was working on it the bartender, Tom Davis, came over.

"Are you in trouble?"

"No."

"I heard what happened last night. To Cody? You saved his life."

"I guess I did."

"Everybody is talking about it."

"Who's everybody, Tom?"

Tom waved his hands helplessly and said, "Everybody. I heard about it this morning while I was walking to work, then again when I got here, and all day long from customers."

"Is that a fact?"

"Yes, sir. You know, I think if you was to get on-stage and sell tickets the way Cody does, you'd make yourself a lot of money."

Clint frowned up at the young man and asked, "Who told you to say that?"

Tom looked bewildered and said, "Nobody. Why?"

"Never mind." He looked at the man again, critically, and then said, "There's something different about you today."

Tom blushed, touched his face, and said, "Yeah, I shaved off the muttonchops."

"That's it."

"How do I look?"

"Younger."

Tom gave Clint a look and said, "See? I told you."

Before Clint could say anything, the young man walked away in a huff. Clint shook his head, laughed to himself, got up and left.

THIRTY-SIX

The killer knew what hotel Buffalo Bill Cody was staying in. The voice had told him. Standing across the street he saw Clint Adams come out, and knew that he had come into some luck. Adams was staying at the same hotel. Before he could successfully kill Cody, he knew he had to get rid of Adams first.

The voice was angry with him last night for killing the whore. He tried to explain how he had been doing the girl a favor by killing her, but the voice didn't want to hear his explanations. Now the only way for him to make things right with the voice was to kill Clint Adams, so he'd have a clear shot at Cody.

He watched Clint Adams walk down the street in the direction of both Huron and Rush streets. He didn't know which one the man was going to, or if he was heading somewhere else, but it didn't matter. He waited a few moments, then stepped out of the doorway he was hiding in and followed.

THIRTY-SEVEN

Clint did as O'Grady suggested and walked directly to the Huron Gun and Hunt Club. There was a man in the front hall sitting at a desk. Clint introduced himself and told the man why he was there.

"Why yes, I know Doctor Kramer," the man said. He had white hair and smooth pink skin. "Yes, I recognize you now from last night, sir. You saved Colonel Cody's life."

"Yes, I did."

"It was a brave thing you did."

"Thank you. Uh, Doctor Kramer? Could you tell me where he lives? Or where his office is?"

"His office and home are in the same building. I don't know the address, but it's across the street and approximately a block and half further on. You can't miss it. He has a huge white shingle out front."

"Thank you."

Clint left the club, crossed the street, and continued on. The man was right. There was a very big white shingle in front of the building that said: DR. EVERETT KRAMER, M.D.

Clint mounted the steps and rang the doorbell. The door was answered by an elderly woman with a pronounced stoop.

"Yes?"

"I'd like to see Doctor Kramer, please?"

"Doctor does not have hours today," she said. "Come back tomorrow, please."

"You don't understand," Clint said. "I'm not a patient. I want to talk to him about a patient."

"What patient is that?"

"William F. Cody."

"Ah, yes," she said, "the emergency that got him out of bed last night."

"That's right."

"Well, come in," she said. "I'll tell Doctor you're here."

He entered and found himself in a cluttered entry foyer. She closed the door and turned to face him.

"You're from the police?"

"No."

She frowned. She had assumed he was a policeman.

"Who are you, then?"

"My name is Clint Adams."

She waited a few moments, then said, "And?"

"I, uh, I'm the man who saved Colonel Cody's life."

She did not look impressed.

"Wait here."

She disappeared into the recesses of the house, leaving Clint to fend for himself among the clutter. There were mismatched pieces of furniture in the foyer, specifically bureaus, chests, coatracks, and bookcases. Piled high were a great many magazines, books, clothing—coats, mufflers, gloves, which hadn't been needed for months now. There was some kind of holder in a corner with a collection of walking canes in it. He went over to examine them. He took one or two out and hefted them, then his hand closed on one with a great silver head in the shape of a lion. It was heavier than the others, and when he examined it he saw why. The head had a catch on it, and then a thin blade slid out of the cane. He didn't have time to check the blade because he heard the woman returning. He pushed the blade back home, heard the catch "catch," and then put the cane back where he got it from. Apparently, there were times when the good doctor felt the need for protection. With the things that had been going on just since he arrived in Chicago, Clint didn't blame the man.

He was standing right where the woman had left him when she returned, but she eyed him suspiciously anyway. It was as if she knew something was out of place, even if it was just a half inch or so.

"Please follow me," she said. "Doctor will see you now."

The killer found himself a doorway across from the doctor's office and settled down to wait. Maybe Clint Adams felt the need for a doctor when he went in, but just a little while after he came out he wouldn't need a doctor at all.

He'd need an undertaker.

THIRTY-EIGHT

The woman took Clint down a hallway that was as equally cluttered as the foyer, and then into an office that was not only crowded but musty. The place smelled as if a window hadn't been opened in months—and it was hot!

Behind a desk sat Doctor Kramer. Clint remembered him from the night before. He looked older today, in his sixties rather than his fifties. Clint found that odd. Last night the man had been trying to throw off the vestiges of sleep. Today he looked wide-awake, but older.

"Doctor, this is Clint Adams."

"Thank you, Amanda."

She nodded, turned, and left.

"Been with me thirty years," Kramer said of the woman.

"That's nice."

"Ugly as sin," Kramer went on, "but she keeps things straight around here."

146

Clint didn't know what to say to that, so he didn't say anything. He also noticed that the doctor, for a man who was elderly, had very thick wrists. He thought the man must have been deceptively strong.

"So what can I do for you? Some sort of injury from last night?"

"No," Clint said, "I feel fine. I'm here about Colonel Cody."

"What about him? He's going to live, if that's what you're worried about. The wound was not as bad as it looked. Once I got the bullet out—"

"I'd like to know what his condition is now. Should he be walking around?"

"Not unless he wants to start bleeding again," Kramer said. "See, that is the main danger here. If he starts to bleed he could bleed to death if not treated, or the wound could become infected—"

Clint realized that the doctor would just keep talking unless he was interrupted.

"So what you're saying is that he should stay indoors for a few days?"

"A week, at the least," Kramer said. "And he should stay in bed most of the time—and the wound has to be cleaned and the bandage changed—"

"So there's no way he should keep his speaking engagements."

"None whatsoever. I strongly advise against it. Why, it would be like—"

"Thank you, Doctor," Clint said. "That's all I wanted to know."

"I'll be over to see him again later today," Kramer said, "but after this he should get someone to clean his wound and change the bandage each day. It's very important that he—"

"I'll tell him, Doctor," Clint said, inching toward the door. "Thank you."

Clint left the office, retraced his steps to the cluttered foyer, where the woman was waiting for him. How had she known that he was leaving?

"This way," she said, and opened the door.

"Thank you."

As he left he noticed again the cane with the silver head, and then he was outside with the woman closing the door firmly behind him.

Across the street the killer saw Clint Adams exit the doctor's house. He was slouching against the wall and stood up straight as Clint came down the steps. He was about to cross the street and follow him when he heard someone call out, "Mr. Adams? Mr. Adams?"

He ducked back into his doorway.

Clint heard the voice calling his name and realized it was coming from ahead of him as he retraced his steps along Rush Street. He looked ahead and saw Howard Billings coming toward him. He was dressed as he had been the last time Clint saw him, replete with bowler hat.

"I'm glad I caught you," Billings said, out of breath. He fell into step with Clint, who never broke stride.

"What can I do for you, Mr. Billings?"

"I spoke to Colonel Cody this morning," Billings said, trying to keep up with Clint's long strides.

"What did he have to say?"

"Well, as I understand it, he intends to go on tomorrow unless, you, uh, that is, unless you agree to replace him."

"What else did he say?"

"That you, uh, refused to do so. Mr. Adams, I'm here to plead for—"

"All right."

"—Colonel Cody. I mean, he's—"

"All right."

"—in no condition—"

"Billings! I said all right!"

"What?"

"You convinced me," Clint said. "I'll do it."

"You will?"

"Yes."

"That's wonderful," the smaller man said. "I'll, uh, make all the arrangements. I'll have a marquee made up with 'the Gunsmith' on it—"

"No," Clint said, "just my name."

"Mr. Adams, if you'll excuse my saying so, this is my business, and we will draw many more people with your, uh, that is, with the name that you have a reputation with—I mean, that is to say, not that your own name isn't respected—"

"Forget it, Billings," Clint said. "Just do it the way you want. Okay?"

"All right. Uh, where will you be later so I can tell you what the arrangements are?"

"I'll be at the hotel," Clint said, "thinking up a bunch of lies."

"What?"

Clint quickened his step and left Billings behind.

"I'll be at the hotel!"

"I'll talk to you later," Billings called, unable to keep up.

Clint waved over his shoulder and kept going.

• • •

The killer was angry. The little man had kept him
from killing Clint Adams, and now that Adams had
reached Michigan Avenue all he could do was follow
him back to the hotel and await another opportunity.

THIRTY-NINE

Clint spent some time in the hotel bar, trying to think of what he would talk about the next day when he made his appearance onstage.

The only other time he had ever been onstage was in St. Louis, when he took a part in a play to try to help catch a killer. He'd been very nervous that night, but at least he had been onstage with other people. Tomorrow he'd be up there all alone, with no one to distract attention away from him. He was already regretting his decision when he got the germ of an idea. He turned it over and over in his mind until he thought he had it figured, and then he left the bar and went to Cody's room.

The same policeman, Foster, was on the door.

"Foster, I'm sorry if I got you in trouble with the lieutenant."

"It's all right," the younger man said. "It wasn't too bad."

"Have you heard anything from Colonel Cody?"

"Not a sound."

"I'll just check on him."

Clint opened the door and stepped inside. As before, the bed was empty and Cody was by the window, staring out.

"You'll be glad to know I've decided to replace you for tomorrow's performances."

"That's no surprise," Cody said, still staring out the window.

"Really? You expected me to agree?"

"I knew you would."

"How could you know that?"

"I'm a good judge of character."

"What do you find so interesting out the window?" Clint demanded.

"Did you know you were followed to the hotel?"

"What?"

Clint crossed the room and joined Cody at the window.

"Across the street, in that doorway underneath the sign—there, see, he popped his head out?"

"I see him."

"And you didn't see him on the street?"

"I guess not."

"Do you recognize him?"

"Can't see him well enough from here."

"Think that might be our man?"

"Maybe he's just a would-be thief."

"Maybe," Cody said, "and maybe that's the son of a bitch who shot me."

"Let's go down there and find out."

Cody moved away from the window with more speed than his injured shoulder should have allowed.

"Where do you think you're going?" Clint asked.

"With you, to face this bastard."

"No, no, no," Clint said, "if you're too injured to go onstage tomorrow you're sure as hell too injured to go downstairs with me. You wait here."

"Well, take my gun, man. You don't even—"

Clint plucked the New Line from behind his back and showed it to Cody.

"That toy?"

"I can hit what I shoot at with this, that's all that matters. Now just wait here and watch."

"You're not going to take that policeman with you, are you?"

Clint stopped to think a moment.

"He's too young," Cody said. "He'll go running out there and scare the man off."

Cody made sense. Neither Foster nor the man in the lobby seemed all that experienced to do anything but stand watch.

"I won't mention anything to him," Clint said.

Cody moved back to the window and looked out.

"He's still there. Hurry up, before he gets impatient, and before it gets too dark."

"I'm going, I'm going."

He tucked the New Line back behind his back, into his belt, and went to the door.

In the hall he said to Foster, "I'm going to go and get him some dinner."

The man nodded.

In point of fact it was already pretty dark outside. The killer wondered if Clint Adams would be coming out again. The voice told him not to risk going into the hotel because there were sure to be police around, but he was sorely tempted. He could slip into the hotel and kill both Adams and Cody—but Cody had to be killed in a certain way, according to the voice. He had to be killed while he was standing up in front of all those people, like last night.

Finally, though, he decided to come back in the morning. Chances were, with the wound he'd inflicted on the man, Cody might not even appear tomorrow, but he was going to have to wait to find that out.

He was hungry, and impatient, and still angry that he had missed his chance at Adams earlier. He decided to forget about the rest of tonight and go back to his hotel, where the voice would speak to him again.

FORTY

It was all Clint could do to keep from running through the lobby, but that would have tipped off the policeman there that something was afoot.

He reached the front door of the hotel and looked out. The doorway across the street was too dark for him to see if the man was still there. With the interior of the hotel well lit, however, the man would surely see him leave.

Clint looked around and spotted the doorman.

"Is there a side door out of the hotel?" he asked.

"Yes, sir. In fact, there's one on each side. If you go right through there . . ."

"Thanks."

Clint went down a carpeted hallway and eventually came to the side door. He went out and worked his way toward the front of the hotel. He peered around the corner, but from here the doorway was even darker.

He moved away from the hotel and crossed the

street as quickly as he could without attracting attention. Now he was on the same side as the man in the doorway. He moved from doorway to doorway, working his way to the one he and Cody had seen the man in. Finally, he was in the next doorway. He removed the gun from his belt, took a deep breath, and then ran to the doorway and leapt in, reaching with one hand and holding the gun out with the other.

The doorway was empty.

The man was gone.

"Shit."

He stepped out of the doorway and looked both ways, but couldn't see anything. He started to cross the street back to the hotel, but something made him look up at Cody's window. He saw a bright light there. Cody had put his lamp in the window and Clint was able to see him clearly. He was pointing frantically. Of course, Cody had been watching, had seen the man leave, and knew which way he had gone. Clint squinted and saw that Cody was pointing to the right—that is, *his* left.

He waved at Cody and started walking to his left. He increased his pace, because he didn't know if the man was walking straight or if he'd turned a corner. He walked two blocks, pausing to look up and down the cross block, but it was too dark to see anything clearly. He went another block, but it was futile. Whoever the man had been, he was gone, and now night had fully fallen.

He turned and started walking back to the hotel, and then heard something behind him. A footfall. Was he coming back? Quickly he ducked into a doorway and waited. The footsteps came closer, speeding up as they did, and then he was there. Clint reached out, grabbed the man from behind, and shoved his gun into his back.

There was a scream, high-pitched, like a woman, but Clint knew it was a man.

"What the hell—" he said, spinning the man around.

The face he saw was that of Howard Billings—a pale, frightened Howard Billings.

"What the hell are you doing here?" Clint demanded.

"Don't kill me, don't kill me!" Billings begged.

"I'm not going to kill you," Clint said, "stop blubbering."

Tears were running down Billing's face and his shoulders were hunched.

Clint released him and put away his gun.

"Calm down."

"You f-frightened me."

"Yeah, well, you scared me pretty good, too."

"I scared you?"

"Did you see anyone on your way here?"

"Uh, no, I didn't see anyone. Is . . . is everything all right?"

"Everything is fine, Mr. Billings. Where were you headed?"

"To the hotel to see you."

"Okay, come on," Clint said, "I'll buy you a drink."

FORTY-ONE

Ten minutes later Clint and Billings were sitting at a table in the bar. Clint had a beer and Billings a whiskey, which he was sipping.

"I'm not much of a drinker," he'd said when Clint ordered the drink.

"Just one, to calm your nerves."

"May I ask what you were doing out there?" Billings asked.

"Cody and I saw someone watching the hotel. We thought it might be the man who shot him."

"I see."

"I'm sorry I scared you, Mr. Billings."

"Please," the man said, "call me Howard. After all, you did almost scare me to death."

"All right, Howard," Clint said. He sipped his beer and then asked, "What were you coming to see me about?"

"Oh, uh, everything is ready for tomorrow. I will have a cab pick you up at two o'clock for the three

158

o'clock performance, and then from there we can get something to eat before we go to the seven o'clock."

"The seven o'clock is at Derek Mills's theater, isn't it?"

"That's right."

"How does he feel about the substitution?"

"He's excited about it," Billings said. "I understand he offered you a chance to do this before the colonel was injured?"

"That's right."

"And you refused him."

"Yes."

"Well, he understands that Colonel Cody is injured, and he's very happy that you are taking his place."

"I'm sure he is."

"Do you know what you'll be doing?" Billings asked.

"Talking."

Billings smiled and said, "Yes, but do you know what you will be talking about?"

"I have an idea."

"May I ask what it is?"

"Why do you have to know that?"

"Well, I don't—"

"Then I'll discuss it with Cody," Clint said. "If he approves, then you'll hear it tomorrow, along with everyone else."

"Well . . . all right, then," Billings said. He looked at the shot glass of whiskey, of which he had finished half, and said, "That is very strong. I feel a little dizzy."

"Maybe you should take a cab home, rather than walk," Clint suggested.

"Yes . . . yes,"Billings said, "I do still feel rather . . . rattled."

Clint stood up and helped Billings to his feet.

"Come on, we'll have the doorman get you a cab."

"Yes, thank you."

Clint walked Billings to the front of the hotel and left him in the care of the doorman.

"I'll see you tomorrow," Clint said to Billings.

"Yes, yes, two o'clock."

"Right."

He left the two men there and went up to Cody's room again. Foster was still there.

"When do you get relieved?" Clint asked.

"In about an hour," Foster said, and yawned.

"Be sure to tell the new man about me, huh? I don't want to get shot."

"I'll tell him, sir. Don't worry."

Clint knocked and then entered. He was just about accosted by Cody before he could close the door behind him.

"Where have you been? Did you get him?"

"No, I didn't," Clint said. "For some reason he left before I got there."

"Yes, I saw that. I saw him walk away, and then I signaled you."

"I went after him, but it was too late—and then I ran into Billings."

"And?"

"And we scared the hell out of each other."

"Where was he going?"

"Here, to see me, to talk about tomorrow."

"Tomorrow . . ." Cody said, as if reminding himself. "Damn it, I thought we had him."

"If that was even him," Clint said. "We don't know that."

"Now we have to wait until he tries again to get him," Cody said.

"Maybe he won't get a chance to try," Clint said. "You're injured. When he sees that you're not performing tomorrow, maybe he'll give up."

"There are two other options," Cody said.

"What are they?"

"First, he might try for me here."

"In which case the police will catch him," Clint said. "What's the second option?"

"That you'll be substituting for me in more ways than one," Cody said.

"You mean—"

Cody nodded.

"Maybe he'll try to kill *you* tomorrow."

FORTY-TWO

It was a sobering thought.

"If he's after you, why should he kill me?" Clint asked.

Cody shrugged.

"Maybe because you saved me last night."

"Are you trying to talk me out of taking your place, now?"

"No," Cody said, "I'm just trying to talk you into being careful. Both venues are larger than the Huron Club was. There will be a lot of people there, so it will be easier for him to hide."

"And then easier to get away."

"You better have a talk with your friend the lieutenant," Cody said. "He should have enough men there to protect you—or at least to catch the bastard after he kills you."

"That'll be a comfort."

"Make sure he has more experienced men than he has here," Cody said. "I don't think that lad outside has even begun to shave yet."

"Hey, he's twenty-eight if he's a day."

"Maybe I'm just gettin' older."

"I talked to Doctor Kramer today."

Cody sat down in the chair by the window, but not in front of the window, so he wouldn't make a target out of himself.

"Oh yeah? What'd he have to say?"

"He wants you in bed for a few days and off your feet for at least a week."

"Ha!" Cody said. "I hope you don't get too comfortable onstage tomorrow, because I should be ready to resume by the day after."

"Bill—"

Cody held his hand up.

"Clint, you and I know more about getting shot than that doctor does," Cody said. "We certainly know more about our own bodies. I'll put my arm in a sling day after tomorrow and be ready."

"To make a target out of yourself again?"

"The only way we're gonna find out who this nut is, is if he tries for you tomorrow or me the next day."

"Maybe he won't try anymore at all. Maybe once was enough for him."

"I doubt it," Cody said. "This is a crazy man. He'd have to be to try to kill me in front of all those people. No, he'll try again. I'm sure of it. You'd better wear your gun tomorrow, and I don't mean that little toy you've got on you now."

"That's a good idea," Clint said.

"It will add to the picture, too," Cody said. "Do you want to borrow one of my buckskin fringe jackets?"

"Uh, no, I don't think so."

"Have you decided what you're gonna do tomorrow?"

"Pretty much."

"Gonna talk about your early days? Maybe some adventures with the Earps or Masterson?"

"No."

"Something later, then," Cody said, "more recent adventures?"

"Nope."

Cody frowned.

"By God, man, what are you gonna talk about?"

"Not what," Clint said. "Who."

"Who? What do you mean, who? Who else could you talk about besides yourself?"

Clint smiled and said, "You."

"Me? Why would you talk about me?"

"Because I'll feel like less of a fool than if I was talking about myself."

"But what do you know about me?"

"Only what I've heard," Clint said, "and what I heard from you last night. That's why you and me are going to have dinner up here together, and you're going to talk to me."

"About what?"

"Stories, Bill, about you and *your* adventures. Maybe even what you would have talked about if you were appearing yourself tomorrow."

"I don't get this," Cody said. "This is a chance to talk about yourself—"

"I don't like talking about myself, Bill," Clint said. "I'm not like you. I can't talk about my adventures, even if I was to lie about them."

"But you can lie about mine?"

"Sure. I can lie about anybody else with no problem. It's lying about myself I don't like."

Cody stared at him and said, "You're the damnedest man. You and Hickok were great friends, I heard."

"We were."

"And yet you're so different. Hickok would talk to anyone who would listen. He'd tell stories about himself, tales taller than anything I could ever think of."

"That was Hickok," Clint said, "and this is me."

Cody thought it over for a few moments, then shrugged—and winced.

"Ouch. When do we start?"

"I'll go downstairs and arrange for a couple of dinners. Beef stew sound okay?"

"Beef stew sounds great."

"Okay," Clint said, "some beef stew, a couple of beers, and a pot of coffee, and we'll be set."

Clint started for the door and Cody said, "Get some coffee for that lad outside the door. I want to make sure he stays awake."

"He's being replaced within the hour," Clint said, "but I'll bring some up for the new man."

As Clint left, Cody peered out the window again. It was dark, and he wondered if the killer was lurking around out there again. He didn't like the idea of a faceless enemy. Come right at me, he thought, that I can handle.

Come right at me, you son of a bitch.

FORTY-THREE

Clint and Cody had a slow dinner together while Cody told him some tall tales.

"Is any of this true?" Clint asked. It was midnight, and he was getting ready to leave.

"There is a germ of truth in every tale I tell, Clint," Cody said. "That's how I can tell them with such conviction."

"Well, I only hope I can tell it with half as much conviction."

"You won't."

"Why do you say that?"

"Because they're my stories, not yours," Cody said. "You'd be able to tell your own stories with much more conviction."

"You mean my own lies."

"Whatever."

They left the dishes on the top of the chest of drawers, and Cody got into bed. In addition to beer, Clint had brought up a bottle of whiskey, and it was only

166

half empty. He decided to take it back to his room with him.

"I'm more tired out just from talkin' to you than I get talkin' to a crowd."

"Why is that?" Clint asked, moving toward the door.

"That's easy," Cody said. "No applause."

Clint clapped a couple of times and then said, "I'll see you in the morning."

He left, exchanging good nights with the policeman who had replaced Foster. His name was Kennedy, and he was older and apparently more experienced.

Clint went down to the second floor, to his own room, and as he entered he sensed another presence in the room. Initially, he thought it would be Pamela Lutz, but when he didn't smell any perfume he took his gun out from behind his back.

"Take it easy," Talbot Roper said. "It's just me."

"Where the hell have you been?" Clint asked, closing the door.

"Gettin' here," Roper said, "and then lyin' low."

"Why?"

"I don't want whoever killed Hannigan to know I'm here," Roper said.

"Do you know who killed Hannigan?" Clint asked.

"Not exactly."

Roper had made himself comfortable, removing his boots and lying on the bed to wait. He had not, however, turned the bed down, but had settled right on top of the bedclothes.

"Why don't you fill me in on everything that's

happened before we talk about what I know?" Roper suggested.

Clint agreed. He sat on a chair and removed his own boots while telling Roper about finding Hannigan and everything that had happened since then.

"So the police don't know anything?"

"They've had some other things to work on," Clint said. He then told Roper about the attack on Cody and the dead prostitutes.

"Jesus," Roper said, "I knew Chicago was a rough city, but this is a little ridiculous."

"I agree."

"I could use a beer."

"This will have to do," Clint said, picking the bottle up from the floor where he'd set it by his feet and tossing it to Roper, who caught it neatly. "I'm worn-out, and I've got to get some sleep. I have to go onstage tomorrow."

"What?"

Clint told Roper about replacing Cody onstage.

"That I've got to see."

"Not if you want to keep a low profile."

"Oh, we'll have Hannigan's killer by then."

"How will we do that?"

"Do you have that letter I gave you for Hannigan?"

"I do."

"Have you read it?"

"No."

"You haven't?" Roper was surprised.

"I didn't figure it was any of my business."

"I've got to admire you, Clint," Roper said. "I would have opened it the minute I found him dead."

"Well, I'll give it to you and you can open it."

Clint took the letter out of his jacket and offered it to Roper.

"I know what's in it," Roper said. "I wrote it. Open it and read it yourself."

Clint withdrew the letter.

"Are you gonna tell me you're not curious about what's in the letter?"

"Oh, I'm curious."

Roper stared at Clint and said, "You really didn't open it?"

"I really didn't."

"Well, go ahead, do it now."

Clint opened the envelope and slid out two pages of neatly handwritten notes. He read it quickly and was surprised by the contents.

"Hannigan sent me a telegram and asked me to check out this doctor. I did and found out that the man had a bad reputation in Denver. In fact, he was accused of some crimes and fled. Apparently, he set up practice here in Chicago under a different name."

"What name?"

"That I don't know. I checked out the name Hannigan gave me, but he never told me the name the man was using here."

"But this is the man's description?" Clint asked.

"It is," Roper said, "right down to an annoying habit he has of talking and talking unless he's interrupted."

Clint read the notes again, then folded them and put them back in the envelope. Now he wished he had opened the letter before.

"What's wrong?"

"I know where this man is."

"Where?"

"I was at his office today. He's the doctor who treated Cody."

"What?" Roper stared at Clint. "I know how you hate coincidence, and this is a big one."

"Maybe not. Hannigan's office is on Rush Street, and this doctor—he goes by the name Kramer—has an office not that far away."

"Well," Roper said, "if you know where he is, we can go get him in the morning."

"There's one thing we've got to watch out for."

"What's that?"

"He looks old and frail, but he's not. Also, he has a cane with a sword in it. I think that's what he must have used to kill Hannigan. In fact, he almost took Hannigan's head off with it."

Roper winced.

"Was he a friend of yours?" Clint asked.

"Hannigan was a colleague. He needed something checked out in Denver and I checked it, but I still don't like to hear that he died like that."

"I've got a question."

"What?"

"Did he ask you to check this doctor out in a telegram?"

"Yes."

"Why did you ask me to bring him the reply?"

"He asked if I could find some way to send the reply without using a telegraph line. I guess he thought the doctor might get wind of it."

"How?"

"You'd have to ask him that, but we can't, so I guess we'll never know."

"So you want to go and pick up the doctor tomorrow?" Clint asked.

"Yes."

"And then what?"

"Take him to the police."

"I think maybe we should take the police with us."

"Do you have someone in mind?"

"Yes," Clint said, and told Roper about Sean O'Grady.

"Sounds like you're gettin' along pretty good with the local police."

"He's a good lawman."

"Okay, then we'll take him with us."

"Let's meet at breakfast and go to the police station together."

"What do you mean, meet at breakfast? I don't have a room."

"Go and get a room."

"There are no rooms available."

"So where are you going to sleep?"

"In this room with you."

"Well, then, you get the floor."

Roper spread his arms and said, "The bed's big enough for both of us."

"Roper, I am not sharing a bed with you. Sleep in the chair, or sleep on the floor, but I'm warning you, get out of my bed. I'm tired and I need some sleep."

"Jesus," Roper said, getting off the bed, "what's makin' you so testy?"

"I'll tell you in the morning. Right now I just want to get to sleep."

"Can I at least have a blanket?"

"Big-time private detective," Clint muttered, taking the blanket off the bed and tossing it to him.

"Good night to you, too."

FORTY-FOUR

In the morning Clint and Roper went downstairs for breakfast. All during the meal Roper complained of a stiff neck.

"Get yourself a room somewhere tonight so you can sleep on a real bed."

"Are you kidding?" Roper said. "Chicago is much too dangerous a place for me. Once we wrap this up, I'm on the next train back to Denver. I'll sleep in my own bed when I get home."

After breakfast they took a cab to the police station and Clint introduced Roper to O'Grady and Folkes.

"We've heard of you," O'Grady said. "What can we do for you?"

"It's about James Hannigan."

Clint and Roper discussed how this would be done, and they decided that Clint should be kept out of it as long as was possible.

Roper explained that he was doing a job for Hannigan involving a doctor in Chicago who may or may not have fled Denver under suspicion. The private detective produced his report, stating that he had been bringing it to Hannigan, and showed it to O'Grady.

"This is about a doctor named Kanter," he said. "Is there a doctor by that name in Chicago?"

"I think I can help there," Clint said.

"How?" O'Grady asked.

"The doctor who took care of Cody the other night? His name is Kramer."

"So?"

"I talked to him yesterday. He has an annoying habit of talking and talking until you interrupt him. He literally will not stop until you cut him off."

"I repeat," O'Grady said, "so?"

"Look at my report," Roper said.

O'Grady looked at it again, obviously having a problem with Roper's handwriting.

"You've got to get somebody to start typewriting your reports, Roper," he said.

"It's an expense I've been tryin' to avoid."

"I see you mention an annoying habit this Doctor Kanter had, similar to the one Clint mentions about Kramer."

"Also the physical description fits."

O'Grady looked at Clint and Roper.

"That's still not much to go on."

"Isn't it enough to question him?"

"I don't think—"

"There's something else."

"What?"

"Kramer has a cane with a sword in it."

O'Grady looked at Folkes.

"Hannigan could have been cut with a sword," the sergeant said.

"It would take a strong man, though."

"I got a good look at Kramer yesterday," Clint said. "He's got wrists like tin cans. I think he's a lot stronger than he looks."

O'Grady thought it over, then looked at his sergeant.

"What do you think, Folkes?"

Folkes shrugged.

"I guess it's worth talking to him."

"Okay," O'Grady said, "let's go talk to the man."

The same old woman who had opened the door for Clint the day before opened it again. She eyed the four men benignly.

"Can I help you?"

"I am Lieutenant O'Grady, this is Sergeant Folkes," O'Grady said. "We'd like to see the doctor."

"He'll be taking patients in about an hour," she said. "If you could come back—"

"I'm sorry, ma'am," O'Grady said, "we're not patients. This is a police matter. I'll have to insist that you let us in."

"Very well."

She backed away and the four men entered, after which she closed the door. Clint looked at the canes and saw that the one with the big silver head was missing.

"Has the doctor been out today?" he asked.

"Yes," she said, "he went for a walk."

"Did he take a cane?"

"He always has a cane—except for the other night, when you people called him out."

"We'll see the doctor now," O'Grady said.

"I'll tell Doctor you're here—"

"Never mind," O'Grady said. "We'll go in unannounced." He looked at Clint and said, "You've been here before. Lead the way."

Clint led them down the hall to the doctor's office. The man was seated behind his desk and looked up in surprise.

"That's him," Roper said.

It was a tack they had agreed to take on the way over: make the doctor think he'd been recognized.

"What is the meaning of this?"

"Doctor Kanter—" O'Grady started.

"My name is Kramer."

"Yes, here it's Kramer," Roper said, "but in Denver it was Kanter."

Kramer blanched.

"I've never been to Denver—"

"He's lying," Roper said. "I saw him."

"What is your name?" Kramer asked O'Grady.

"Lieutenant O'Grady, sir," the policeman said. "Did you know a James Hannigan?"

"I do not know anyone by that name."

"Sure you do," Roper said. "He was a detective who found out about you when one of your dissatisfied patients went to him and hired him. You discovered that he knew about you, and you killed him."

"That's a lie."

"Doctor Kramer," O'Grady said, "we'll have to ask you to come with us to answer a few questions."

"Take him to Hannigan's office," Clint suggested, as planned. "Show him to the witnesses."

"Witnesses?" Kramer asked, going pale again.

"Just one or two," Clint said.

Folkes approached the doctor and said, "Just come with us, sir."

Clint saw the doctor reach for something behind his desk as Folkes neared him, then he saw a flash of silver.

"Look out!" he shouted. He reached out and pulled Folkes back just as Kramer swung his sword cane. The blade cut through Folkes's clothing and tore his flesh, but the wound was not serious.

"Damn!" he shouted.

O'Grady drew his gun and shouted, "Stop!"

"I'll kill you all!" Kramer shouted, coming around the desk.

O'Grady said, "Stop!" again, but fired a split second later. He was taking no chances. The bullet struck Kramer in the chest, but he kept coming.

Clint pulled his gun from behind his back and fired, hitting the doctor in the stomach, but the man continued to advance. He was a *lot* stronger than he looked.

O'Grady fired again, and so did Clint, but this time Clint put his bullet between the doctor's eyes. The man stopped short and stood there for a moment. Blood began to seep from the wound, down his nose until it dripped from the end, and then he fell.

"Sergeant!" O'Grady called.

"I'm cut," Folkes said, both hands pressed to his chest, "but not bad, thanks to Mr. Adams."

Roper looked down at the doctor, then at Clint and said, "I guess I'm on the next train to Denver."

FORTY-FIVE

From backstage Clint looked out at the crowd. He had already performed at the smaller theater at three that afternoon, and it had gone well. He told one of Cody's stories, pacing the stage as Cody had done. In the audience he saw Pamela Lutz and her husband Philip; Sean O'Grady; Howard Billings; Tom Davis, from the Drake; and Derek Mills. He figured Mills was checking his performance in the hopes that it would go well and ease his mind for the later performance.

Now he was in Mills's theater, which was much bigger. There seemed to be a veritable sea of faces out there, waiting for him.

"How are you feeling?" Mills asked from behind him.

"Nervous," Clint admitted.

"You'll be fine."

Clint didn't tell him that he was nervous because no one had tried to shoot him earlier in the day. That

177

only made it seem more likely that, if it was to happen, it would be tonight. How was he going to pick the man out from among all those people before the shot was fired?

Clint was pleased to see O'Grady there. The man had closed the Hannigan case with Dr. Kramer's death and was looking into the possibility that the same sword might have been used to kill the prostitutes. That investigation would have to be put on hold temporarily, though. Bowing to pressure from his superiors, O'Grady was concentrating first on the Buffalo Bill Cody case. Clint didn't think that Kramer was the killer of the girls, but he thought that would be obvious when the next one was killed. Hopefully both he and Cody would be gone from Chicago by then.

So with the Hannigan case closed, O'Grady had extra men at the hotel watching Cody, and men outside the theater here while he himself was in the audience. Still, how would that help Clint? At best they would catch the killer after he shot Clint.

Clint knew he was going to have to go out there on that stage and try to look at every face. The would-be killer, if he was there, would at least have to be close enough to get a clear shot. Clint decided to concentrate only on the first ten rows.

"It's time," Derek Mills said.

The killer watched from his seat in row eleven as the curtain came up and Clint Adams stepped out. The voice had told him to kill Adams, and that would clear the way for Cody to be next. However, it had also told him not to do it that afternoon in the small theater, but this evening in the larger one.

And no more girls, the voice said.

No more.

Clint walked out onstage with his modified Colt strapped to his hip. He'd worn it that afternoon for the first time since his arrival in Chicago, and although he felt like a target out there, it was also the most comfortable he'd felt in days.

He chose to tell the same story he'd used that afternoon. According to Derek Mills, the crowd was almost certain to be a different one, with very few exceptions.

One of those exceptions was Lieutenant Sean O'Grady. Clint could see the policeman clearly. The man was spending more time watching the crowd than the show, which he appreciated. He himself, while reciting the story told to him by Cody—complete with "embellishments"—studied as many of the people in the first ten rows as he could. He did not see anyone who looked like the killer.

There were several points during the story which had brought applause that afternoon. It happened again this evening, and Clint prepared himself for something to possibly happen. When it didn't, he started to think that maybe the killer would not go after him. Just because he had saved Cody's life and replaced him didn't necessarily mean he would become a target as well.

As he passed the halfway point he felt that the only danger left was at the end. He'd gotten a standing ovation that afternoon—that is, Cody's story had—so there was every reason to believe it would happen again this evening. With everyone standing and applauding, it would be a perfect time for the killer to strike.

As he approached the end of the evening, Clint decided to expand his field of inspection from ten rows to a dozen. He was reciting the last line as he swept row eleven with his eyes, and as he spoke his last word he saw him. The man was seated right at the end of row eleven and Clint was sure it was the same man he had bumped into outside of Hannigan's office.

As the applause began and people started to stand, he kept his eyes on the man. What could he do if the man started shooting? He had two options, drop to the floor or return fire—or, a third, fire first.

As he bowed he kept his eyes on the man, who didn't seem to realize he'd been spotted. In fact, the man looked like he was in a trance.

As he bowed a second time he saw the gun, and his action was instinctive. There was never the thought of dropping to the floor or taking cover. The man lifted his gun and pointed it, and no one noticed because their eyes were on the stage. Not even Lieutenant O'Grady could see what was going on.

Only Clint.

In one swift movement he drew and fired into the audience. Some people screamed, but most of them seemed to think it was part of the show.

Sean O'Grady followed Clint's aim and saw the bullet strike the man. Fervently, he hoped that Clint Adams had not made a mistake. When he got to the fallen man and saw the gun, he breathed a sigh of relief.

When a woman saw the blood she began to scream stridently, and that started another screaming.

From the stage Clint saw O'Grady wave his men

forward. They had been standing at the back of the stage. Apparently, they were good at their jobs, because they kept a riot from happening.

Clint holstered his gun and got off the stage, vowing never to step onto another one again.

"And they found *what* in his room?" Cody asked.

"Pieces of . . . well, the girls. He had taken them with him and kept them."

"So it wasn't the doctor who killed the women, but the same madman who shot me."

"Right."

"What are the chances of that?"

"Slim," O'Grady said.

They were in Cody's room, the same night of the shooting. O'Grady and Clint had returned to the hotel late, but wanted to tell Cody what happened, so they woke him.

"Coincidence," Cody said.

Clint winced.

"I hate coincidences," he said, "and Chicago seems too full of them. Cody, you're going to have to find someone else to go on for you in your next performance. I'm catching the next train west."

"What about your friend? The newspaperman? Wasn't he the reason you came to Chicago?"

"One of the reasons," Clint said, "and we've completed our business. I was smart enough to say no to him and stick to it. The other reason I came was because I felt Chicago would be an interesting place."

"And so it is," Cody said.

"Real interesting," O'Grady said.

"Too damned interesting," Clint said. "I'm going back to the uncivilized West . . . where it's safe!"

Watch for

**THE WILD WOMEN OF
GLITTER GULCH**

163rd novel in the exciting GUNSMITH
series from Jove

Coming in July!

If you enjoyed this book, subscribe now and get...

TWO FREE

A $7.00 VALUE—

If you would like to read more of the very best, most exciting, adventurous, action-packed Westerns being published today, you'll want to subscribe to True Value's Western Home Subscription Service.

Each month the editors of True Value will select the 6 very best Westerns from America's leading publishers for special readers like you. You'll be able to preview these new titles as soon as they are published, *FREE* for ten days with no obligation!

TWO FREE BOOKS

When you subscribe, we'll send you your first month's shipment of the newest and best 6 Westerns for you to preview. With your first shipment, two of these books will be yours as our introductory gift to you absolutely *FREE* (a $7.00 value), regardless of what you decide to do. If you like them, as much as we think you will, keep all six books but pay for just 4 at the low subscriber rate of just $2.75 each. If you decide to return them, keep 2 of the titles as our gift. No obligation.

Special Subscriber Savings

When you become a True Value subscriber you'll save money several ways. First, all regular monthly selections will be billed at the low subscriber price of just $2.75 each. That's at least a savings of $4.50 each month below the publishers price. Second, there is never any shipping, handling or other hidden charges—*Free home delivery.* What's more there is no minimum number of books you must buy, you may return any selection for full credit and you can cancel your subscription at any time. A TRUE VALUE!

J. R. ROBERTS

THE
GUNSMITH